The New Girl

Note to the Reader

'The experience of Syrian refugees prompted me to write this book. I felt compelled to try to find a way to show children and young readers how incredibly difficult some people's lives can be. I met Sarra al Hariri, a Syrian refugee, through the Irish Refugee Council in Dublin, and her story inspired me further.

Readers everywhere tell me that my stories make them think and feel. I hope that the same compassion shines through *The New Girl* for a whole new generation of readers as, through fiction, they get to walk a mile in someone else's shoes and grow to understand the importance of empathy and kindness in life.'

– Sinéad

'When I read *The New Girl*, I could relate so much to the character of Safa. She has the same feelings, fears and problems that I had when I arrived in Ireland. I want everyone to read this beautiful and important book because it will raise awareness of how refugees deserve to be treated.'

– Sarra

Sinéad MORIARTY

The New Girl

Gill Books

Gill Books
Hume Avenue
Park West
Dublin 12
www.gillbooks.ie

Gill Books is an imprint of M.H. Gill and Co.

First published in 2021. This paperback edition published in 2022.
9780717195053

Design and print origination by O'K Graphic Design, Dublin
Edited by Esther Ní Dhonnacha
Proofread by Jane Rogers
Printed by Clays Ltd, Suffolk

The paper used in this book comes from the wood pulp of sustainably
managed forests.

5 4 3 2

For my beautiful friend Sarra al-Hariri
and for all refugees who have had to flee
their homes in search of safety

CHAPTER ONE

Ruby

Ruby knew it was wrong to hate your brother, but sometimes she did hate Robbie. Like, really really hate him, and then she'd feel guilty about it and sick to her stomach. Hating was bad. She knew that, but sometimes Robbie was hard to love.

Orla walked in front of her on the way to school, talking loudly into her phone. 'I know ... OMG, like, no way ... I, like, have to get that new fake tan – it's amazing.'

Ruby thought her older sister sounded ridiculous. She sounded like a fake American from LA, when she was just a stupid Irish teenager. And the last thing she needed was more fake tan. That morning at breakfast Dad had said that Orla looked like she'd been rolled in cheesy Doritos.

Ruby and her mum laughed. Then Orla told her dad that he was too old to know what was cool these days. Dad said he was pretty sure going out with an orange face and body wasn't in fashion.

Ruby loved having a laugh with her mum and dad, but they didn't do it much any more. Robbie took up all of Mum and Dad's time and energy, so they never really had much time for the girls.

And they must have laughed too loudly because Robbie started having a tantrum. He threw his arms and legs around, flung his bowl on the floor and started screaming. Ruby hated her little brother for ruining her precious moment with her mum and dad. Robbie kind of ruined everything.

Orla yapped away on her phone while Ruby dragged her heels. There was a new girl starting in the class today. Miss Ingle had told them the previous Friday. Ruby didn't want any new girls in her class. She felt anxious around new people. She didn't want them to find out about Robbie and feel sorry for her or, worse, avoid her like some people did.

Whenever Amber and Chrissie saw her out in town with Robbie, they always crossed the road and pretended they hadn't seen her. It hurt. It hurt that no one else in her class had a brother with disabilities. No one understood how hard it was and now, some new girl was going to join the class and she'd soon find out about Ruby's little brother.

When she arrived at school, Ruby hung her coat up in her locker and looked around the classroom for Denise and Clara. They were chatting in the corner. Ruby wandered over to them. 'Hi, guys.'

'Oh hey,' Denise said.

'We're just talking about the new girl,' Clara said.

'Is she from around here?' Ruby asked.

'No!' Denise said. 'Not at all. I heard Miss Ingle talking to Mrs Roberts in the corridor on Friday when I was getting my football gear out of my locker and she said something about how Miss Ingle must make sure that her class were extra nice to the refugee girl.'

'Refugee?' Ruby paused. 'Like, from one of those

mad countries that people have to run away from?'

Denise shrugged. 'I guess so.'

'She's probably from Syria,' Clara said. Clara was the girl in the class who knew about everything. Ruby didn't know how she did it. She had a really small head, but inside was a massive brain full of knowledge. Then again, Clara's mum was really smart too, and she was an only child. Ruby dreamed of being an only child. The thought of having Mum and Dad all to herself was bliss.

Clara never came to school with no lunch because her mum had been up all night with Robbie and was asleep on the couch at breakfast time, worn out from yet another sleepless night. Clara never had to remind her mum ten zillion times about everything – books, parent–teacher meetings, sports days, Christmas concerts ... Clara's mum never arrived late or didn't turn up at all to school events. Clara's uniform was always washed and ironed and smelt of fresh flowers. Ruby had Orla's hand-me-down uniform and the elbows on her jumper were almost worn through.

'Where's Syria?' Denise asked.

Clara sighed. 'Seriously, girls, do you never watch the news?'

Ruby looked at Denise and they both said, 'No.'

'You should. My mum says it's very important to be informed about what's going on in the world and too many girls are glued to their phones looking at random celebrities on Instagram.'

Ruby was a bit afraid of Clara's mum, Annabelle. She was very smart and had set up the biggest law firm in town. Annabelle had gone back to work after Clara's dad died of cancer when Clara was only a baby. Annabelle had worked super hard and now her law firm was the biggest and the best. She was always dressed in navy, grey or black trouser suits and she sounded like a dictionary when she spoke.

Besides, Ruby liked looking at what celebrities were wearing and doing on Instagram. It was nice to disappear into other people's glamorous lives and get away from her own. She never watched the news because it was full of bad stories and she didn't want to hear them.

'So where is Syria, then, Einstein?' Denise asked.

'It's in the Middle East, beside Turkey and Iraq.'

Ruby wasn't sure where the Middle East was, but her granny had been to Turkey once and brought her back a big box of Turkish Delight. Ruby thought the sweets were gross but had to pretend to like them so she wouldn't hurt her granny's feelings. The sweets had white dust all over them and were all squishy and tasted disgusting. Ruby felt sorry for people living in Turkey if that was their best national sweet.

She had definitely heard of Syria and not in a good way. 'Isn't there a war there or something?'

'Yes, a terrible war that has been going on since 2011. There are nearly six million Syrian refugees.'

'What? That's more than the whole population of Ireland,' Denise gasped.

'Way more,' Clara said.

'It must be hard to leave your country,' Ruby said.

'Not if there's bombs going off and a big war,' Denise noted. 'I mean, Ireland's not great and it rains a lot but still, it's, like, peaceful and stuff.'

Ruby supposed she was right. Still, though, if Syria was near Turkey, the new girl would be frozen in Ireland. Ruby's granny said that Turkey was boiling hot and she had spent the whole ten days of her holiday sweating in the shade, eating ice-cream.

From across the room, where Amber and Chrissie were sitting, they heard a loud voice say, 'Refugee?

Ewwww, we don't want them in our school. They come from really poor places and don't even know how to read or eat with knives and forks. Most of them are criminals. They'll steal all our stuff. Watch your bags, girls! Don't leave anything out or it'll be gone.'

Clara clenched her fists. 'God, I hate Amber.'

But Ruby knew Clara wouldn't tell Amber that she was an idiot. Everyone was a bit scared of Amber because she was a year older than them and she had three older sisters in the school. If Amber decided she didn't like you, she and her sisters would make your life hell. Rumour had it that her sister Irene had flushed another girl's head down the loo and put dead spiders in her sandwiches, all because the girl had refused to give Amber's sister her Mars bar.

The classroom door opened. All twenty-four heads spun around. There stood Miss Ingle and a small girl with thick dark hair and huge brown eyes.

'Girls, I want you to welcome Safa to our class,' Miss Ingle announced.

Ruby sank down in her seat. She knew Safa would be put beside her because she was the odd one out. Although Denise and Clara were her friends, they were each other's best friend and she was the 'other' friend.

Whenever it came to pairs, they always chose each other. Ruby pretended she didn't care, but sometimes she did.

Right now, she really did. She didn't want the refugee girl beside her. What if Amber was right? What if she stole Ruby's things? Ruby stuffed her favourite glitter pen into her bag.

Safa sat down quietly beside Ruby and pulled a copybook and a plain blue pen out of her backpack.

'Ruby will show you the ropes and help you settle in this week, won't you, Ruby?' Miss Ingle made it sound like a question, but it wasn't. It was an order. She had that serious tone in her voice, like, a 'Don't mess with me, Ruby, do what I say' tone. Ruby knew she'd have to obey or be in trouble.

'Yes, Miss Ingle,' she muttered. Damn, now she was stuck with the stupid refugee for the whole week.

CHAPTER TWO

Safa

Safa felt naked without her hijab. She'd only been wearing it for a year, but she'd got used to it. It felt like a protection around her head. It made her feel safe and secure, but Mrs Roberts, the headmistress, said that no headscarves were allowed inside the school.

When Safa had translated this news to her mother, she had looked sad but shrugged. She told Safa to just say yes to everything the headmistress said. She wanted Safa to go to this school. It was supposed to be the best one in the town – or so the woman from the local refugee council said.

It wasn't as nice as Safa's old school back in Syria. But then again, that was gone. A bomb dropped right in the middle of it one Sunday morning. Boom. The beautiful building collapsed into rubble.

Safa and her friends had cried when they saw it. That was the day her family decided to leave Syria. Her father had said, 'Enough. If they are now bombing schools, we cannot live in this country any more. We have to go.'

Two weeks later they had left Syria and begun the long and awful journey to Ireland. Safa tried not to think about it. She tried to block out the bad memories. But at night, when she dreamed, the images came back to her. She woke up most nights sweating with her heart racing. She'd sit bolt upright in her bed, panting. Then she'd realise that it was only a dream and feel so relieved. But then she'd remember that it wasn't a dream; those terrible things had actually happened.

The counsellor at the emergency centre they were put into when they first arrived in Ireland kept saying to her, 'Try to remember, you're safe now, Safa, you're safe. If you feel afraid, repeat the sentence over and over: "I am safe now."'

But it was very hard to feel safe when you'd felt afraid for so long. Safa's mother, Rima, pretended not to be afraid any more, but Safa could see she still was. Yesterday when they were walking home from the shops a car horn had beeped loudly and her mother had almost jumped out of her skin. She'd dropped her bag of shopping on the road and everything had spilled out.

Safa had had to chase a mango that rolled down the hill. When she'd got back to her mother, she had still been shaking. But then Rima had done that thing she'd been doing for over a year now: she had fake-smiled and placed the palm of her hand on Safa's cheek. 'It's OK, Habibti.'

But it wasn't OK. None of it was OK.

They had been in Ireland for eight months now. When they'd first arrived in Ireland, they were stuck in the emergency centre in Mosney with other refugees from all over the world. But now they had a little house in Wexford. The house was nice, but it rained all the time and the sky was grey all the time and it was cold, and the food tasted awful and Safa just wanted to go home. She really, really wanted to go back to Syria and for everything to be normal again.

But she had to pretend too. It made her mother feel better if Safa just smiled and said, 'Yes, Mama, everything is fine.'

After putting all the shopping back into the bags, they'd walked back to the house in silence, each lost in her own thoughts and memories.

Now Safa sat very still and tried to listen to every word Miss Ingle was saying. Her English was very good, thanks to her father being an English teacher and talking to her in English since she was born. But even though she was fluent in English, the Irish accent was hard to understand sometimes. Like when they said 'water', they didn't pronounce the 't'. They said 'washer'. And 'tomato' was 'tomasho'. It had taken Safa a few weeks to realise that Irish people pronounced 't' like 'sh'.

Safa had also missed a year of school while in the refugee camps and she was desperate to catch up. One of the last things her father, Baba, had said to her was 'Safa, education is freedom.'

Safa wasn't so sure about that; Baba was educated and he wasn't free. He was still stuck in Greece. The Red Cross had given them two visas, one for Mama and one for Safa. They said that they would make sure that her dad would get one as soon as possible and follow them over, but he still hadn't. Safa had helped Mama to write to the Minister for Justice to apply for family reunification, which meant that Baba would be able to come to Ireland and live with them, but they had heard nothing back yet. Safa prayed that she would be reunited with her father soon. She missed him every second of every day.

Safa leaned forward to listen to Miss Ingle. The girl beside her, Ruby, was fidgeting with a pen that had a mermaid in the top part. When she put it one way the mermaid had a tail, but when she moved it the other way, the tail disappeared and she had legs.

Safa watched as the mermaid changed form. The girl looked sideways and caught Safa watching.

Safa took a deep breath and decided to break the silence between them. 'I like your pen,' she whispered.

'Well you can't have it and don't even think about nicking it.' Ruby shoved the pen into her pencil case and zipped it up.

Safa looked down at her hands and willed herself not to cry. Why would this girl think she wanted to steal her pen? All she did was say she liked it.

Safa closed her eyes to stop the tears from falling. She thought back to her bright, sunny classroom in Syria and her three best friends, Sarra, Amira and Taqwa. She missed them so much. She wondered what had happened to them.

They had stayed behind. Their families believed things had to get better. They were wrong; things had got worse. She prayed that they were safe and unhurt.

They had laughed so much together. Always making jokes, dancing, singing and laughing. Safa missed laughter. She couldn't remember the last time she'd really laughed. Life was so serious now, there was no reason to laugh.

Tears escaped from her closed eyes and rolled down her cheeks. She heard the girl beside her gasp. Safa opened her eyes.

Ruby was staring at her, her big green eyes wide with fear. 'God, I'm sorry, I didn't mean to make you cry. Please stop. Miss Ingle will kill me if she thinks I've upset you,' she whispered.

Safa wiped the tears away with the corner of her scratchy grey school jumper. She hated the feel of it on her skin.

'Are you OK now?' Ruby asked.

Safa nodded.

'Look, if you want the pen that badly, take it.' Ruby pulled the mermaid pen out of the pencil case and handed it to Safa.

Safa shook her head. 'I don't want your pen. I just said I liked it. I have never stolen anything in my life.'

'Seriously, nothing?' Ruby seemed surprised. 'Not even chocolate from your mum's bag?'

Safa smiled. 'My mum doesn't eat chocolate.'

Ruby grinned. 'Mine lives on it.'

They sat side by side in silence, then Ruby asked, 'How come your English is so good? Do they speak English in Syria? I thought you spoke some other language?'

Safa nodded. 'We speak Arabic in Syria, but my dad is an English teacher – he went to university in the UK – so from the time I was very small, he spoke English to me.'

'You sound very posh when you speak – like a posh English person. I'm rubbish at languages. I'm the worst in the class at Irish.'

'I've never studied Irish, but it sounds so lovely when it's spoken.'

Ruby looked at her as if she was mad. 'Lovely? It's a total nightmare. It's super hard to learn and you don't spell it like it sounds. You should try to get out of learning it.'

Safa shook her head. 'I want to do everything that the other girls in the class do. I want to learn as much as I can.'

Ruby raised her eyebrows. 'Wow, you're keen. Miss Ingle is going to love you. I hate school.'

Safa bristled. Was this girl seriously saying these words? Didn't she know how lucky she was? 'My school was bombed to the ground. You are so lucky to be able to go to school in a peaceful country. My dad says that education is freedom.'

'Jeez, keep your knickers on. I was just saying I don't love school.'

'Well, you should be happy that you can go.'

Ruby sighed and stared at her mermaid pen. Safa tried to calm down. She needed to keep her frustration in check, or she'd never make friends. She had to remember that these girls hadn't experienced or seen what she had. They hadn't had to leave their country and friends behind. They took their peaceful lives for granted.

The bell rang for break. Ruby got up and rushed towards the door.

'Ruby? Haven't you forgotten someone?' Miss Ingle said.

Ruby turned around slowly. She beckoned Safa to follow her out. Two other girls walked with them down the corridor towards the front door. They introduced themselves as Denise and Clara.

Safa stopped to grab her coat.

'You don't need that,' Denise said. 'It's warm today.'

Warm! Safa had been freezing walking to school earlier.

'She's from Syria, for God's sake – it's roasting over there.' Clara told Denise.

'I do find it cold here,' Safa said.

'Cold, rainy and crap,' Denise added. 'If I lived in a hot country, I don't care what was going on, I'd stay and have a tan all year round.'

'You don't tan, you burn,' Ruby grinned at her friend. 'We all do.'

Clara's face reddened. 'For God's sake, guys, she ran away from a war.' Turning towards Safa, she said, 'Please excuse my ignorant friends. They don't watch the news.'

'It's OK, I'd never heard of Ireland before I came here,' Safa admitted.

'You sound like the queen when you speak – so posh!' Denise said. 'Do all your family speak English?'

'It's just me and my mum here. She doesn't speak much English so I translate for her, but she's been getting lessons, so she's improving.'

'Are you an only child?' Clara asked.

Safa nodded.

'Me too! Great, I was the only one in the class until now. It's just my mum and me at home too.'

'Hi, dork.' A teenage girl strutted across the yard to them.

'What are you doing over here in the junior school yard?' Ruby hissed.

'Relax, I need to borrow money for lunch.'

'I only have two euros.'

'That'll do.' The older girl held out her hand. Noticing Safa, she asked, 'Who's your new pal?'

'This is Safa. Safa, this is my sister, Orla,' Ruby mumbled.

'Your cool, drop-dead gorgeous, almost-sixteen-year-old sister Orla.' Orla blew a chewing gum bubble out of her mouth. 'Are you the refugee I heard about?' she asked.

'Yes, I'm from Syria.'

'Cool. Is that your natural tan or are you wearing fake? It looks real.' Safa struggled to understand this older girl. She spoke so quickly and chewed gum at the same time. It was hard to follow what she was saying.

She didn't look like Ruby at all. Ruby had brown hair and green eyes; her sister had dyed blonde hair and blue eyes. She was wearing lots of make-up around her eyes that made her look a bit like a clown.

'Leave her alone, Orla. It's her first day,' Ruby said.

'I need to know if that's fake, 'cause if it is, I want it.'

'It's not fake, it's her skin colour. Syria is beside Turkey. It's boiling hot all the time,' Denise said.

'Well, not all the time. In the winter it can get quite cold,' Safa said.

Orla flicked her hair back. 'Well, your tan will fade soon enough in this dump of a country. And my advice to you, Afra or whatever your name is, is to stay away from this lot. They are the super nerds of fifth class. You don't want to be associated with them. Seriously.

No one will speak to you if they think you're friendly with my geeky sister.'

'Sod off, Orla,' Ruby hissed.

Orla ignored her. 'So listen, Ruby, you're going to have to look after Robbie today while Mum is out. I can't do it.'

Ruby's face went bright red. 'No way,' she hissed. 'It's your turn.'

Safa wondered who Robbie was.

'I can't do it. I'm meeting Jack in Starbucks after school.'

'I am not doing it.' Ruby's fists were clenched. 'It's not fair. I've done the last three Mondays.' Ruby was close to tears. Safa felt bad for her.

'Well I won't be home, so he'll starve.' Orla walked off.

Ruby roughly wiped the tears in her eyes away. 'You are so lucky,' she said to Clara and Safa. 'I wish every day that I was an only child.'

The other girls looked at each other but said nothing. Safa was very curious to know who Robbie was and why no one wanted to go home and look after him.

CHAPTER THREE

Ruby

Ruby had to go to the bathroom to calm down. She was so furious with Orla for dumping Robbie on her again. It wasn't fair. She kicked the wall of the school toilet and locked herself into a cubicle to cry.

Mondays were the worst day in Ruby's week. First of all, the weekend was over and she had to go back to school, and second of all, when she got home, she had to give Robbie his dinner while her mum went to yoga. It was the only time her mum had to herself. The doctor said she had to have some time to herself or she'd break.

Ruby wasn't supposed to know about this, but she'd heard her mum and dad talking about it. Her dad had said, 'Fiona, if you fall apart, we'll all go down. You have to take time out for yourself. The doctor said so. He said you'll break otherwise.'

A week later her mum had signed up to yoga classes in the local church hall and she'd been doing them now for six weeks. So every Monday, Orla and Ruby were supposed to take it in turns to feed Robbie while Mum was out.

But so far, Ruby had done it five times and Orla only once. Ruby had hoped her mum would notice, but when she got home on Mondays her mum was always standing at the door in her tracksuit, dying to get out. She'd say a quick hello and then rush past Ruby down to the town hall.

Ruby wanted to complain, to give out about Orla, to say it wasn't fair, but she didn't. Mum needed this break and Ruby didn't want to ruin it by causing trouble or complaining.

She had said it to her dad last week and he said he'd have a word with Orla, but then Robbie had spiked his finger with a fork and screamed the house down. It had been a tiny cut but when he saw the blood he had freaked out.

Dad had forgotten after that and Ruby didn't want to bother him. Not bothering Mum and Dad was what Ruby tried to do, all the time. It was also what everyone told her to do – constantly. 'Don't bother your mum and dad,' her granny said, the occupational therapist said, the speech therapist said ... Everyone was very clear that she was not to bother her parents.

But it was hard sometimes. Really hard. Last week she'd needed help with her maths for her weekly test, but she couldn't ask her dad because he'd fallen asleep on the couch. After Mum had had to give up work to look after Robbie, Dad had to drive the taxi way more than before and he was always tired these days. He had black rings under his eyes. But Ruby had really needed help. So she went to her mum.

'Not now, Ruby,' she'd said. She had been reading Robbie his favourite book – *The Gruffalo* – and she couldn't stop, or he'd have a tantrum.

So she'd tried Orla.

'Forget about your stupid maths. Put this on my back.' Orla had handed Ruby a mitt and a bottle of fake tan.

'Orla, I need help. I failed my test last week and I'll fail again this week.'

'Who cares? Maths is boring and it's not as if you're going to be a maths professor or whatever. Don't streak my tan – rub it in evenly or I'll kill you.'

Ruby had sighed and rubbed the tan into her sister's back.

She had failed her maths test again. Miss Ingle had taken her aside and told her that she really needed to 'pull up her socks'. Ruby had bitten her lip really hard to stop herself crying.

Miss Ingle must have noticed because her voice then went all gentle and she'd said, 'I know things are difficult at home, but you must try to really focus on your maths this year.'

Ruby had been afraid to open her mouth in case a big sob came out, so she'd just nodded and hurried out of the classroom.

Safa was waiting in the bathroom when Ruby came out of the cubicle. She didn't ask her if she was OK or anything, just silently handed her a tissue and patted her on the arm.

'Denise told me Robbie is your brother and he has some problems, is that right?' Safa said.

Ruby felt her face redden; she hated talking about Robbie. 'He has learning disabilities and he uses a wheelchair,' she muttered.

'That must be difficult for you.'

Ruby wiped her eyes with the tissue. 'Yeah, it is, but he's very sweet sometimes too,' she added.

She always felt she had to add that part. It was true too. For all the times Robbie was really annoying, he *could* be sweet too. And it wasn't his fault he was born that way. He didn't get enough oxygen in his brain and that was why he was different.

When he was calm, Ruby read him books or watched his favourite TV shows with him. He loved *Peppa Pig*. Ruby found it really boring and thought Peppa and all her squeaky-voiced friends were so annoying. But Robbie liked it, so she watched the episodes over and over and over again. When the theme song came on, Ruby would oink and snort along and Robbie would smile and shake his legs and arms. Moments like that were when Ruby liked her brother, loved him even.

Safa looked at Ruby with her big brown eyes but said nothing. It should have been awkward but for some reason it wasn't. Ruby could see that somehow, Safa 'got it'. There was nothing to say, so she didn't fill the air with pointless words or comments.

'We better get back to class,' Ruby said.

Safa followed her out. They walked in silence and then Ruby said, 'We have gym after lunch – did you bring in your shorts?'

Safa stopped. 'What is gym?'

'It's gym class. Sports.'

Safa frowned. 'What sports will we play today?'

'Well, this term it's football.'

Safa looked relieved. 'I like football. I learned how to play it in the refugee camp in Greece. We had a good coach. She was from Somalia and she was very good at football.'

'Cool. Mr Kowalski is mad into his football. He really wants us to win the cup this year.'

'But I can't wear shorts.'

'Why not?'

'Because I must be covered.'

'Shorts do cover you.' What was Safa on about?

'My legs and arms must be covered.'

'But you'll be boiling! We're playing in the gym hall because it's raining.'

'I'm used to being warm.'

'But it's silly. Just put on a T-shirt and shorts like all of us.'

'I can't.'

'Why?'

'It's against my religion. I'm not supposed to play sport in front of men either, but Mama said that because we live here now I can as long as I'm covered.'

'But you live in a boiling hot country – how can you go around in long sleeves and trousers all the time? That's just mad.'

Safa shrugged. 'It's what Muslim girls do. We also cover our heads with a hijab, but Mrs Roberts said I could only wear it coming to and from school but not inside. I am finding that very difficult.'

Ruby looked at Safa's long, thick, shiny black hair. Why would she want to cover it? It was gorgeous. 'What's a hijab?'

'It's a scarf that covers your head.'

'I don't get it! Why would you have to cover your hair? It's amazing.'

'It's what Muslim girls do. It's part of our culture and tradition.'

'So, you're telling me that you have to go around with a covered head and body all the time?'

'Not all the time. When I'm at home, I can uncover my head and wear what I want.'

Ruby didn't understand. Safa was gorgeous. She had amazing hair and beautiful brown skin. She should be walking around in shorts, swishing her hair about all the time.

'Look, you have customs that are different to mine. When you make your communion and dress up in a big white dress and a veil – that seemed very strange to me when I saw the girls dressed up in May. They looked as if they were dressed like mini brides.'

Ruby had never thought about it that way. She'd hated her communion dress. It was Orla's old one and was too tight and was all poufy and flouncy. Ruby had wanted a long, straight dress and no veil. But Robbie was in hospital with a lung infection and Mum was too stressed to take her shopping and besides, money was tight, so she'd just shut up and worn Orla's poxy dress and veil and pretended she didn't mind, although she really did mind, a lot.

In the pictures Ruby did look like a little bride. It was a bit strange if you thought about it. 'Yeah, but that's only for one day, and believe me, I never wanted to wear the dress or veil again. You have to do this every day.'

Safa shrugged. 'It's just what we do. It's my "normal". Like for a lot of girls in Ireland, wearing fake tan is normal. This also seems very strange to me. Why would you want to paint your body brown every day?'

Ruby did think that all the fake tan Orla used was ridiculous. She overdid it and often ended up looking kind of orange. But all her friends did it too. All teenagers seemed to. 'I guess we all do things that seem weird to each other.'

Safa gave a little smile. 'My father always used to say, "If we were all the same, life would be very dull."'

'Your dad sounds clever.'

'He is.'

Ruby could sense a sadness when Safa mentioned her dad. It was the way she felt when she said Robbie's name. 'Is your dad here too? You said it was just your mum and you, so ...' Dammit, maybe he'd been killed in the bomb at her school that she mentioned. Oh no, she shouldn't have asked. What if he was dead? *Please don't let him be dead in a big bomb.*

Safa's eyes clouded over. 'No, he is in Greece. He couldn't get a visa to come here. But we're hoping and praying that he will come soon.'

'Do Catholic prayers count? Like, if I pray will it help?'

Safa smiled. 'All prayers count. Thank you.'

Ruby wasn't sure about God any more. If God was all kind and loving, why was Robbie the way he was? When he was first born, four years ago, Ruby had prayed every day that he'd get better. But he didn't. Still, it was worth a few prayers to try and help Safa get her dad back. She'd try her best.

When Ruby got home, her mum was waiting at the front door.

'He's watching *Peppa Pig*. There's twenty minutes left and then his dinner is in the oven. Make sure none of the peas roll down and touch the chicken.'

'OK. Have a good time.'

'Thanks, love, you're a good girl.' Fiona bent down and gave Ruby a hug. It was the first hug she'd had in a while.

Mum was always either with Robbie or falling asleep all over the house. Ruby had once found her asleep on the loo! Since Robbie arrived her mum and dad were constantly exhausted. Before he came along, they used to do loads of stuff together. Now ... well, now they had no time and no energy. Whenever they'd tried a 'fun family outing' it always ended up with Robbie freaking out or breaking something or shouting the place down. Mum and Dad would get really stressed and they'd all have to leave the restaurant, cinema, park – wherever they were – and go home. They never really bothered any more. Sometimes, on special occasions, her mum would take her out to the café down the road for a hot chocolate and a bun, but they were always rushing to get back or the phone would ring and Dad would say Robbie wanted Mum NOW.

Mum turned around when she got to the end of the little path outside their house. 'Wasn't Orla supposed to look after Robbie today?'

'Yeah, but we swapped. It's fine.'

'OK, well, make sure she does next week.'

'Sure,' Ruby said. She was delighted that her mum had actually noticed, but she knew that by the time she got back from yoga she'd have forgotten all about it.

Ruby put her backpack down in the hall and went in to see Robbie. He was strapped into his wheelchair and was humming along to the *Peppa* theme tune. At least he was calm.

Ruby went in and sat down on the couch beside him. She watched his little face light up as Peppa jumped in a muddy puddle. She sat back and hummed along with him. Not too loudly, though; you had to get the volume just right. Orla had joined in once and sang too loudly, which had led to a massive meltdown that had lasted almost two hours.

As the episode finished Robbie said, 'Again,' which was one of the only words he could say. He could also say, 'Kank you', 'Peese', 'Bye', 'No' (which he said a lot), 'Es' and 'I dove you.'

Suzie, the speech therapist, was very happy with Robbie's progress in speaking, but Ruby had heard her dad say, 'Fifty quid, three times a week for a year, and he has about five words!'

But Mum had shushed him and told him that Suzie was the 'best in town' and that any words at all were progress. The fact that Robbie could communicate at all was kind of a miracle, Mum said. 'Remember, Frank, the doctors didn't think he'd be able to speak at all.'

Dad hadn't looked convinced, but he'd dropped the subject and handed over the fifty euro to pay Suzie the speech therapist.

'We're going to have dinner now, yum,' Ruby said to her little brother.

He shook his head from side to side. 'No. Again.'

'Mum made you chicken, rice and peas, your favourite.' Ruby knew she had to try to gently persuade him to eat. You had to tread very softly with Robbie.

'No. Again.'

'OK, dinner first and then Peppa, OK?'

'No. Again!'

Robbie's hand began to twitch. Ruby took a deep breath. She had to stay calm. 'Come on, Robbie, we'll get your Peppa Pig sippy cup and your Peppa spoon, OK? I'll put the purple juice you like in your cup,' Ruby said.

Robbie looked at her and blinked. He didn't say no. So, very slowly, Ruby turned his wheelchair around and wheeled him into the kitchen. Everything had to be done slowly and carefully or Robbie could fly off the handle.

She pushed the chair up to the kitchen table and filled his Peppa cup with Ribena. 'Now, there's your juice and I'll get your dinner.'

Robbie grabbed the handles on the sides of the cup and sucked noisily. Ruby got his plate from the warming drawer under the oven and placed it carefully on the table.

But just as she put it down, a pea rolled sideways and touched the chicken. Robbie stared at it and then he began to scream.

Within seconds his legs and arms were thrashing about, his dinner was upside down on the kitchen floor and his sippy cup had been flung across the room.

'It's OK, Robbie, calm down. It's OK.'

'No no no no no no no!' he yelled.

Ruby bent down to pick the food up and then got a cloth to wipe the floor while Robbie had his tantrum. There was no calming him down when he was like this. He had to tire himself out.

Eventually, after Ruby had cleaned the floor and wiped down the walls that were covered in Ribena, she turned back to him. 'Do you want sweeties, Robbie?' she asked as he paused in his shouting to catch his breath.

He wasn't really allowed sweets. Sugar made him hyper, but right now Ruby didn't care. She just wanted him to put something into his mouth and stop freaking out before her mum got home. She knew that if Mum saw Robbie upset, she'd never go to yoga again and Ruby really, really didn't want her mum to break. She wanted her to go to yoga and have her time out.

Ruby shook a mini-packet of Skittles in front of Robbie. He stopped shouting. She poured a handful onto the table. He looked at the colours. He popped a purple one into his mouth.

Ruby watched as the sugar soaked into his tongue. He slowly began to smile. 'Yum yum,' he said.

'Yes, yum yum.' Ruby smiled back as relief flooded through her body. It was going to be OK.

She'd just have to pretend that Robbie had eaten his dinner and hide it at the bottom of the bin. She'd hide the Skittles packet too.

CHAPTER FOUR

Safa

When Safa came out of school and walked towards the big gates, Mama was waiting for her. As she walked towards her, Safa took out her hijab and tied it around her head. She felt better once it was on.

Mama stood apart from the other mothers, standing alone while they all stood in clusters. Lots of the mothers were wearing tight exercise clothes. Some had dogs tied to leads beside them. Some had work suits on, some were in jeans and one was wearing a really short miniskirt that barely covered her bum.

Safa's mum looked old compared to the other mums. Her face was lined. The lines of worry, stress and pain. You could read Mama's life on her face, Safa thought.

But then she saw Safa and smiled and Safa felt all warm inside. Mama's face lit up and her brown eyes radiated love. She put out her arms and Safa ran into them. She nestled her head into Mama's shoulder and inhaled her familiar smell of spices and lavender.

'How was your first day, Habibti?'

'It was fine.' Safa wasn't going to tell her mother that she had spent the day being stared and pointed at. That she felt like an outsider, 'other than', different. That she wasn't sure if she'd ever fit in. She wasn't sure if she wanted to fit in. Irish girls were so different. They talked so fast and their conversations seemed silly and pointless.

The only person Safa felt a little bit comfortable with was Ruby. But when the bell had rung at three, Ruby had grabbed her backpack and raced out of the classroom without even saying goodbye to Safa.

She didn't tell her mother that the girls had sniggered when she came to football wearing a tracksuit and long-sleeved top.

What she did say was 'I did well in football, Mama. I saved two goals.'

'Good for you. Did you find the schoolwork difficult?'

'Not really.' In fact, Safa had been surprised at how easy she had found it. Her father had made sure that she kept up with her schoolwork in the camp in Greece. He had taught her maths and English and history and geography and science every day. 'Baba's lessons really helped. I think I know more than most of the other kids, but there is a girl called Clara who is very smart.'

Mama hugged her. 'Baba always said you were the brightest girl in school. I know you will continue to be. You have a curious mind and a good memory; that's all you need to do well in school. I'm proud of you.'

Safa smiled, the first real smile all day. She linked her mother's arm and cuddled in closer to her. Mama was her safe place. With Mama beside her she knew she'd be OK. 'What's for dinner?' Safa asked.

'Always about the food,' Mama laughed. 'I am making your favourite – mahshi and dawood basha and baklava for dessert.'

Safa clapped her hands. 'Yum! Thank you, Mama.'

'It's to celebrate your first day in school and the beginning of the rest of your life.' Mama smiled at her.

'Did you go to class today too?' Safa asked.

Her mother looked away guiltily.

'Mama?'

'I didn't feel like it. English is so hard to learn. I wanted to cook you a special meal and I had to go to six shops to try to find the ingredients.'

Safa sighed. Her mother's English was still pretty bad. If she didn't go to class, she'd never get better. She was supposed to go to class for two hours every morning, but she kept skipping it. Safa really wanted Mama to get better at English so she could make friends and so that Safa didn't have to translate all the time. It was tiring having to do the talking for two people.

But she didn't want to argue with her mother, especially as she had gone to so much trouble to cook all her favourite things. So Safa squeezed her mother's arm and just said, 'OK, Mama, you can go tomorrow.'

When they got home, Safa took off her hijab and changed into sweatpants and a T-shirt. Compared to the emergency centre, the house was nice, and Safa was really happy to have her own bedroom, but she hated the furniture. Big, ugly black couches and chairs and a brown carpet that was scratchy under your feet. Her bedroom carpet was a bright green and the walls were painted mint green, which Safa really didn't like. She'd asked Mama if she could paint it a different colour but Mama had said no. 'We are very lucky to have been given this house – we mustn't change anything.'

Safa felt better now she was in her soft tracksuit and T-shirt. She hung her scratchy school jumper on the back of the chair in front of her small desk. *One day,* she thought, *I'm going to buy my own house and I'm going to paint my bedroom walls a beautiful lilac and have a cream carpet and a big bed covered in fluffy purple cushions.*

Safa slipped her bare feet into her slippers and went downstairs to the small kitchen to get a snack. Mama had made hummus and Safa dipped warm pitta bread into it and savoured the flavours. The hummus you got in the shops in Ireland was gross. It tasted awful. Mama's hummus was the best.

Safa sat back in her chair and felt her body relax. She was home. She didn't have to concentrate on what people were saying; she didn't have to pretend not to notice or mind the staring.

She had found the noise of school hard to take too. Since they had had to leave Syria and since all the awful things that had happened on the way to Ireland, Safa couldn't handle lots of noise. It made her feel panicky. School was full of noise: scraping chairs, shouting, chatter, loud laughing, lockers banging open and shut, doors slamming … it was non-stop noise that bounced and echoed off the walls and hurt her ears. When she felt the panic rising, Safa would dig her nails into the palms of her hands and close her eyes. She'd count her breathes, in for five, out for five, in for five, out for five, to try to control her breathing. It usually helped to slow down her racing heart. The counsellor in the refugee camp in Greece had taught her the technique and it did help.

Safa chewed the pitta and let the taste of home bring her back to sunny days eating in the garden of their house with the smell of jasmine filling her nose. She could see Baba sitting there, reading the newspaper, with his glasses perched on the end of his nose, stroking his beard absentmindedly as he caught up with world politics.

She could see Mama singing along to the radio in the kitchen and little furry Adira sitting on Safa's lap, purring.

Safa pushed the image aside. It hurt to think of her father and Adira. She had named her cat Adira because it meant 'strong'. Adira was strong, and brave, but not strong enough. Not strong enough to survive a bomb. Safa's stomach hurt. She didn't feel hungry any more.

She left the kitchen and went up to her room. She lay on her bed and pulled out the photo of Baba holding Adira. Safa kissed the photo of her father and her cat and laid her head on the pillow. She felt completely exhausted. It had been a long first day. She was glad school was over. But she also knew she had to go back tomorrow and try to fit in.

Would she ever fit in here? She didn't think so. *Never mind*, she thought, *I just need to work hard in school, get a good job and earn lots of money so I can buy a big house in Syria for my parents, when the war is over, and we go home.*

Safa closed her eyes as the tiredness of the day overcame her.

CHAPTER FIVE

Ruby

Ruby was in a deep sleep when she heard the shriek. She reckoned the whole neighbourhood heard it.

'I'm going to kill him. I swear, he's dead this time!' Orla screamed.

'Keep your voice down,' Mum hissed.

'What in the name of God is going on?' Dad ran up the stairs.

Ruby sat up and rubbed her eyes. The door of the

bedroom she shared with her sister was wide open and Orla was standing in the corridor holding her ruined mascara.

'He's wrecked it. I left it on the bathroom sink and he grabbed it when my back was turned. This is the third one this month. I'm sick of it. I hate him. He's a little –'

'Stop it.' Mum grabbed Orla's arm and squeezed.

'What did he wreck?' Dad asked.

'My Benefit They're Real!'

'What in the name of God is she talking about?' Dad looked at Mum.

'Her new mascara,' Mum explained.

Orla held up the crushed mascara brush. Robbie had completely ruined it. Ruby felt sorry for Orla. Her sister had paid a lot of money for that mascara and last week Robbie had taken her MAC lipstick from the kitchen table and drawn all over his wheelchair with it, ruining that too.

'He doesn't mean it, love,' Mum said. 'You need to keep things away from him, where he can't reach.'

'I hate him, Mum, I really hate him,' Orla said, as tears ran down her cheeks.

Ruby couldn't believe her sister had said the words out loud.

'Stop that now,' Dad said. 'It's only a bit of make-up.'

Orla turned to her dad, her face flushed with anger. 'It's not just make-up. It's everything. Since he came along everything is different. You're never here because you're working all the time to pay for his therapies, Mum's always sleeping, crying or with him and all he does is destroy things. I wish he'd never been born.'

'You nasty, selfish girl!' Mum screamed at Orla.

Ruby gasped; Mum never screamed. Orla was shocked. Ruby could see her sister was blinking back tears.

Mum was shaking. 'I'm sorry, Orla, but you cannot say that about your brother. It's not his fault. He can't help it. He was –'

'Born that way. Yeah, I know, Mum, I've heard it a million times. I don't care what you say. I hate him.' Orla turned on her heel and ran into the bathroom, slamming the door shut.

Dad reached out to put his arm around Mum, but she shrugged him off and went into Robbie's room.

Dad turned to Ruby. With a sad smile he said, 'Lively start to the day. Would you like breakfast, love?'

Ruby nodded. She slipped her hand into her father's as they headed downstairs. He squeezed it. 'It'll be OK, don't worry, pet,' Dad said. 'It'll all calm down.'

Ruby nodded, but she knew it was a lie. It might calm down for a bit, but soon enough Robbie would break or ruin something else and Orla would go mad again. It happened all the time.

In the kitchen, Dad opened the cupboard. 'Oh dear, we seem to be out of cereal and bread. I'll have to pop down to the shops.' He rubbed his tired-looking eyes.

Dad had just come in from driving the taxi all night. Ruby didn't want him to have to go to the shops. 'It's OK, Dad, I'm not hungry,' she lied. Her stomach rumbled.

Dad smiled at her. 'You know what, love, why don't you throw on your uniform and I'll take you and your sister out for breakfast? I need something to eat before I go to sleep anyway.'

'Really?' Ruby couldn't believe it. Dad never did this. Breakfast out with him would be so cool. She wished it was just her and not Orla too, but still, it would be so nice.

She ran upstairs. Orla was standing in front of the mirror in their bedroom, putting make-up on. She was crying. When she saw Ruby, Orla quickly wiped away her tears.

'Hurry, Dad's taking us out for breakfast. Quick, before he changes his mind or falls asleep.' Ruby was panting from racing up the stairs.

Orla grabbed her uniform, threw it on and the two sisters were downstairs two minutes later.

As they walked down the road to the local café the knot in Ruby's stomach faded away. The argument was over. Here she was with her dad, actually going out for breakfast. This was such a treat.

In the café, they sat down and Dad said they could order anything they wanted.

'Really? Even pancakes with Nutella?' Ruby asked.

Dad smiled, a tired smile. 'Yes, pet, just for today.'

'Cool, thanks.'

Ruby ordered her pancakes. Orla ordered scrambled eggs on gluten-free toast. She wasn't allergic to gluten; she just thought it was cool. Ruby thought it was ridiculous, but she said nothing because she didn't want to start an argument. Dad ordered decaf coffee and toast.

When the food came the girls tucked in. Dad sipped his coffee and then said, 'Look, girls, I want to talk to you about Robbie.'

Ruby stopped chewing. Oh no, was Dad going to give out to Orla and ruin this lovely breakfast?

Dad rubbed his eyes. 'I know it's hard. I know that the last four years have changed a lot for all of us. But your mum and I are doing our best and we need you to help us out. Robbie is … well, he's a lot of work but he's our Robbie. He's my son and your brother and he tries, he really does. He just doesn't understand things the way other kids do. And to be honest a lot of four-year-olds break things. But what I want to say is that Robbie is going to be with us for the rest of our lives and we have to try to make the best of it and work together as a team.' Dad looked at Orla. 'I need you to help your mum, Orla, not make things difficult for her. I know you're frustrated but if we push against each other it'll make things so much harder. I'm asking you both to be as helpful as you can.'

Orla looked down at her plate and sighed. 'I'll try, but it's not easy, Dad.'

Dad reached over and patted her hand. 'I know, pet, but try harder.'

He looked at Ruby and smiled. 'I know you're doing your best, Ruby. You're always helping out. Keep it up.'

He squeezed her shoulder and Ruby beamed up at him. So he did notice how hard she tried to be nice to Robbie. He did know that it was hard, and he did see that she was doing her best. It made her feel all warm inside.

She was about to tell Dad about Safa, the new refugee in the class, and how she had been asked to look after her, but Dad's eyes began to close. He stood up. 'I'm sorry, girls, I have to get some sleep. That fifteen-hour shift has wiped me out. Be good in school. I'll see you later.'

Dad paid the bill and waved goodbye from the door. Ruby finished up her pancakes.

Orla pushed her food around her plate. 'I remember when Dad had loads of energy and used to take us to the park to play football and mess around on the trampoline with us and … well, now he's just knackered all the time.'

Ruby nodded. She remembered too.

Orla looked out the window. 'Look, there's your refugee friend. Are you looking after her today too?'

'I have to mind her for the whole week,' Ruby grumbled.

'Is she weird?'

Ruby shrugged. 'No, she seems OK.'

'Well, you like weirdos. Clara's a nerd and Denise is like a boy. All she does is play football.'

'Thanks a lot. They're actually my friends.'

'You're the Goon Squad. It's embarrassing for me to have such a nerd as a sister. It's bad for my image.'

Ruby rolled her eyes. Orla was obsessed with her 'image'. How she looked, who she was friends with, what she wore ... everything.

Orla pulled a lip gloss out of her bag and began to apply it to her lips. 'Conor Levy asked me out.' She waited for Ruby to react. Ruby didn't have a clue who Conor Levy was. 'Conor Levy is the hottest guy at St Gabriel's. Everyone wants to go out with him, but apparently he likes *me*. He sent me a text yesterday. I'm meeting him after school on Friday.' Orla beamed.

'Is he a nice person?' Ruby asked.

'Are you serious? I've just told you he's the hottest guy in the whole of St Gabriel's. Who cares if he's nice or not? He's so fit.'

'I think nice matters,' Ruby said.

'You're such a nerd. You're going to end up with a dorky guy who's really "nice" and boring.'

Ruby stood up and picked up her bag. There was no point in arguing with her sister. Besides, if they didn't leave now, they'd be late for school. 'Come on,' she said.

Orla looked down at her phone. 'Go ahead, I'm not walking with you. I'm waiting for Karen. She's on her way. Go on, quickly, or you might be one second late for precious school.'

Ruby left the café and headed for school. Another day looking after Safa. Why did she always end up looking after people? At home it was Robbie and now at school it was Safa. It would be nice if, someday, someone looked after her for a change.

CHAPTER SIX

Safa

Safa tried to follow the words but the way Miss Ingle pronounced the words and the way they were written was completely different. This Irish language was very difficult.

Ruby was looking out the window, not listening at all.

Safa nudged her gently. 'Sorry, but where are we on the page? I'm lost.'

Ruby shrugged. 'I don't know. I hate Irish. It's really

hard and boring and no one outside Ireland speaks it anyway.'

'But it's your national language,' Safa said.

'Yeah, but we all speak English. Hardly anyone speaks Irish at home.'

'I'd want to learn my national language.'

'Well, I'm rubbish at languages so what's the point?'

'Baba, my father, says that learning a new language is excellent for the brain. It helps it to expand. You are exercising a muscle.'

Ruby looked at her as if she was mad. 'There are way better muscles to exercise.'

'What do you like?'

'Drama.'

'Acting?'

'Doing plays and acting and singing too, I guess.'

'That's great. Is the class doing a play this year?'

'Yes, a musical.'

'What musical?'

'We don't know yet.'

'Will you be hoping for a big part?'

Ruby blushed and looked down. 'I dunno, whatever. We'll see.'

'I hope you get one. I'm not good at acting at all.'

'Yeah, but you're good at everything else,' Ruby said. 'Even football. I think Denise was a bit surprised that you were so good. She's used to being the best. She has four older brothers who she plays with all the time. She wants to be a professional footballer when she's older.'

'She is very good – and she's a striker, and I'm only good at being a goalie, so she doesn't have to worry about me taking her place.'

'I hate being in goal. It's scary.'

Safa smiled. Being a goalie was the least scary thing in the world. Being smuggled out of your country in a dark truck packed with people was scary. Being put on a small, overcrowded boat in the middle of the sea when you couldn't swim was scary. Not knowing if you were ever going to see your Baba again was scary. Being a goalie was nothing. 'I don't mind it. I was always the goalie in the camp in Greece and then in Mosney too.'

Ruby looked at her. 'Was the camp like actual camping with tents and blow-up beds and stuff?'

Safa shook her head. It amazed her that these girls seemed to have no idea what was going on in the world. How could they not know about the millions of refugees who had had to escape from war? Did they not listen to the news, or talk to their parents? The only person who seemed to know anything was Clara. 'No, it was a refugee camp. We didn't have a tent – we had a plastic sheet held up by four poles. It was overcrowded and we had to queue for three hours for breakfast, three hours for lunch and three hours for dinner.'

Ruby's mouth fell open. 'So you basically spent the whole day queuing for food?'

'Yes, and the food was awful.'

'That sucks.'

Miss Ingle clapped her hands. 'Quiet at the back, please. Safa, if you need to ask a question just raise your hand. I know Irish is new to you. I'm here to help.'

Clara raised her hand. 'Miss Ingle, shouldn't Safa be exempt from having to learn Irish?'

'She could be excused from learning it but Safa has asked to remain with us for our Irish lessons so she can learn.'

Twenty-four heads snapped around.

'Are you mental?'

'Are you nuts?'

'Are you mad in the head?'

No one could understand why Safa wanted to learn another language if she didn't have to.

'My father says education is freedom. I want freedom,' Safa said.

'Freedom?' Amber snorted. 'Learning Irish isn't going to give you freedom. I think you need to see a doctor.'

Safa felt anger rise up inside her. She tried to control it. Mama always said that if you spoke in anger you lost the argument. You had to stay calm to get your point across. She remembered the words Baba had used when he was explaining to her how important it was to learn. She used her father's words now. 'My father told me that freedom is very precious when it is ripped away from you and you have to run away in the middle of the night from your home, your friends and your family. Freedom is the ability to live in your own country in peace. Freedom is being able to go to school without turning up to find your school has been bombed to the ground. Freedom is knowing you will have food to eat, clean water to drink, a place to sleep. Freedom is being with your family. Freedom is knowing you will see your father again. Freedom is getting a good education so that you can help your family and others never to have to go through what you have been through.'

Silence. The class stared at her. Safa's heart was pounding. She hadn't meant to say so much, but she was so angry with Amber. Beside her, Safa felt Ruby's hand slip into hers and squeeze it.

'Well said!' Clara shouted.

'Beautifully put. Thank you, Safa,' Miss Ingle said. 'I think we can all learn a lot from what Safa has just said. Now, back to page twenty-one.'

'I'd love this school to be bombed. It'd be the best day ever,' Amber muttered under her breath.

'What a freak. "Freedom is … freedom is …"' lecturing us,' Chrissie whispered.

Ruby leaned in closer to Safa. 'Just ignore them. They are total idiots. I am too. I never thought about what you've been through. I'm sorry.'

Safa squeezed Ruby's hand back. 'How could you know? I could never have imagined that my life would change overnight from perfect to a nightmare. But it's better now. I like Ireland. People here are very kind to us.'

'Most of the people.' Ruby grinned. 'Some are total idiots.'

Safa smiled. 'There are plenty of idiots in Syria too.'

They giggled.

CHAPTER SEVEN

Ruby

Mr Parson, the drama teacher, held up his hands.

'Drumroll, please,' he said.

The class all tapped their feet on the floor to make a sound like a drumroll.

'This year, our Christmas musical will be' – he paused for dramatic effect – '*The Wizard of Oz.*'

There were some oohs, some aahs and some boos from the class.

Ignoring the boos, Mr Parson told them, 'Auditions will take place next week. Don't worry, everyone will have something to do. If you don't get a part in the actual play then you'll be helping backstage.'

Ruby clasped her hands together under her desk. She loved that movie and Dorothy was an amazing part. She wanted to play her so badly. She'd have to watch the movie and study the words and music really well so that she was perfectly prepared for the auditions.

Ruby loved acting. She loved disappearing into a character and pretending to be someone else. She loved the way it took you out of your own life and into someone else's. Drama was by miles her favourite class and the only one she was good at.

She'd got a major role in the fourth-class production of *The Lion King* last year and somehow was able to remember all her lines, even though there were loads of them. She was also quite a good singer. Amber was a better singer, but she was a rubbish actress, so Ruby had got the role of Nala in the play and it was amazing.

The costumes were incredible. She had really looked like a lioness. Orla had helped her do her make-up, which was a miracle.

She'd told her mum and dad a million times about

the date it was on and they swore they would come. 'Nothing will stop us,' they had said.

But then Robbie had got pneumonia and they'd had to go to hospital with him and they hadn't seen her. Orla had videoed some of it on her phone, but it was rubbish and when Mum and Dad had watched it and tried to be all positive about it Ruby had wanted to cry. They hadn't seen her starring on her big night. They'd missed it. They missed everything and it was always because of Robbie.

Ruby wasn't going to get her hopes up this year; there was no point. Her parents would promise to come and then not turn up, or they would turn up and then fall asleep, like they had when she was in third class at the Christmas carols. Her dad had actually snored his way through. It was so embarrassing.

Safa looked over at Ruby. 'I hope you get the main part,' she whispered.

Ruby reddened. 'Oh, I probably won't, but thanks.'

It was Ruby's last official day minding Safa. One full week was over. It hadn't been that bad, actually. Safa was OK. A bit serious and way too into her schoolwork, but she was nice and she hadn't stolen any of Ruby's things.

Denise and Clara liked her too. Clara asked a lot of questions, though. Ruby could see that sometimes Safa didn't want to talk about the war in Syria and what it was like to be a refugee. But Clara was relentless. She'd obviously been going home and talking to her mum about it and then Googling facts and coming back into school with more complicated questions.

At lunchtime, they sat together, and Clara started again. 'So I read that since March 2011, fighting in Syria has killed half a million people, injured more than one million, and forced over twelve million people from their homes.' Clara sounded like Wikipedia when she came out with her facts and figures. Ruby didn't know how she remembered it all. She obviously had a big melon-sized brain and Ruby had a small pea-sized brain.

'Twelve million? That's like three times the population of Ireland!' Denise was shocked.

'Are any of your cousins or friends from home living in Ireland?' Clara asked.

Safa shook her head.

'None?' Clara insisted.

'Stop asking,' Denise hissed. 'Maybe they're D – E – A – D.'

'Safa can spell,' Ruby snapped.

'Sorry,' Denise said, looking embarrassed.

'It's OK,' said Safa. 'Some of my family were killed, an uncle and aunt and three cousins. Also, my grandparents on my father's side.'

'I'm so sorry,' Ruby said.

'Me too,' Denise said.

'Me three,' Clara said. 'But you're safe here. Ireland is a very peaceful country.'

'Hopefully your dad will get here soon,' Denise said.

'I hope so. We're still waiting for him to get his papers.'

'I hope he gets them soon,' Ruby said. She felt a bit sick looking at Safa's sad face. Safa tried to smile but Ruby could see the memories of home and of her father hurt her. She decided to change the subject. 'Orla has a big date today.'

'With who?' Denise asked.

'Some guy called Conor Levy in St Gabriel's school.'

'OMG!' Denise exclaimed. 'He's in my brother David's class. He's, like, a total football star. Apparently, every girl in town likes him.'

Ruby sighed. 'Well she's hyper about it. She got up at half six this morning to wash and curl her hair and put on her make-up and she made me do her fake tan last night.'

In fact, Orla had come down the stairs humming. Dad had looked shocked. 'Is she sick?' he asked Ruby.

'No, she's got a date.'

'I knew something was going on – she's never in a good mood!'

Orla came into the kitchen.

'I hear you have a date,' Dad said.

Orla spun around. 'Ruby!'

'What? He asked me why you were in a good mood.'

'So who's the lucky boy, then? Does he have any idea what he's in for?'

'Very funny, Dad. I'm not telling you his name because you'll just start all that – "I think I know his dad, he used to play football with me," or "I knew his mother's cousin … blah blah blah."'

'I'd like to know the name of the boy who is taking you out.'

'He's not taking me out, we're just meeting up after school. Jeez, don't make a big deal out of it.'

Dad picked up his glasses and peered at Orla. 'If you don't mind my saying, love, you've gone a bit overboard with the tan and the make-up. You look like you've rolled in mud and then stuck spiders on your eyelids.'

Orla glared at him. Ruby tried not to laugh.

'Dad, you are the last person in the world I would take fashion advice from. Ever.' Orla stormed out of the kitchen and went to put on even more make-up.

'She looks ridiculous. I presume Mrs Oliver will go mad when she sees her arriving into school with all that muck on her face,' Dad said.

'I think she tries to stop them but all the older girls wear make-up now. They get notes from their parents saying they have to wear it because they have spots and the spots make them depressed and they need make-up to cover up.'

'Are you serious?' Dad was shocked.

'Yep.' Ruby shovelled a spoon of cornflakes into her mouth. 'Orla told me.'

'But she doesn't have a letter, so I presume she'll get told to take it off,' Dad said.

Ruby filled her mouth with cornflakes, so she didn't have to answer. She knew Orla had faked a letter from her parents saying she needed to wear make-up because of her spots, even though Orla barely had any spots. Mum and Dad were so taken up with Robbie that they didn't really keep up with what was going on with Orla at all.

By the time Ruby had finished chewing her mouthful of cornflakes, Dad was asleep at the table. All these extra shifts he was working were wearing him out.

Ruby was worried about him. She was worried he'd fall asleep at the wheel and crash the taxi.

Clara crunched her apple loudly, while Denise bit into her second ham and cheese roll.

'Did this boy not come to your house to ask your parents' permission to take Orla out and show commitment?' Safa asked.

Ruby, Denise and Clara burst out laughing.

'Come to our house? No way. Are you mad?' Ruby said.

'Commitment? You only commit when you want to get married,' Denise said.

'In my country a boy has to come to ask the parents before a girl can go out with him alone. They have to show commitment.'

'Orla would rather die than have a boy come to our madhouse,' Ruby said.

'My brothers would never go and talk to a girl's parents before asking her out. That would be, like, way too serious,' Denise laughed.

Safa shrugged. 'I think it shows that they care.'

'Look,' Clara raised her hands. 'Safa comes from a different culture and we should respect that.'

Ruby was getting a bit sick of Clara's lectures on Syria and Safa's culture. 'We know Safa comes from Syria and they do things differently. It's just weird, that's all.'

'Well she probably thinks the fact that Orla goes out with loads of boys is weird,' said Clara.

'Orla doesn't go out with loads of boys. She's only had a few boyfriends.' Ruby defended her sister. She didn't like Clara being all judgemental.

'Different strokes for different folks,' Denise said. 'That's what my mum always says. Come on, let's play football. Safa, will you go in goal?'

Safa and Denise walked over to the playing field. Ruby and Clara walked behind them.

'I didn't mean to slag Orla. I was just saying.'

'Well, it didn't sound very nice.'

'Sorry,' Clara said.

'It's OK.'

Clara bit down on her thumbnail. It was bitten down to the skin. Ruby thought it was strange. Clara seemed so strong and confident, but she bit her nails, which was a sign of nerves. Ruby's mum said that sometimes even people who seemed confident weren't. She also reminded Ruby how hard it was on Clara to have never known her dad and that it was something that Clara probably thought about, and was sad about, a lot.

Ruby, herself, had been thinking about something a lot, and now she had the opportunity to talk to Clara about it alone. 'You know the way your mum is really intelligent?'

'Yes?' Clara chewed her nail.

'Well, do you think she might be able to help get Safa's dad to Ireland so he can live here with her?'

Clara took her thumb out of her mouth. 'My mum is a lawyer for people setting up businesses and stuff.

She doesn't do refugee papers and visas and all that kind of thing.'

'Oh, I thought lawyers could do anything that was to do with the law and government and stuff.'

'No, different lawyers do different things.'

Ruby's shoulders drooped. 'Oh well, maybe her dad will get here soon.'

'I could ask my mum, though. She might know who in the government deals with refugees and visas and all that.'

'Will you?'

'Sure.'

'That would be great.' Ruby watched as Denise pelted the ball towards the goal. Safa dived sideways and saved it.

Ruby cheered. Safa looked over and smiled, a real smile. Ruby felt warm inside. Even though it had only been a week, Safa was beginning to feel like a friend.

CHAPTER EIGHT

Safa

Safa approached the receptionist at the medical clinic.

'Hello, I need to see a doctor. Well, actually my mother does.'

'Doctor Jennings can see you in about half an hour,' the receptionist said.

'Is he a man?' Safa asked.

'Yes,' the receptionist said.

'We can't see a man. It has to be a woman doctor.'

'Well, there are no female doctors free this morning. They're all booked up.'

Safa swallowed. 'Is there any way you could squeeze us in? My mother is feeling very unwell.'

The receptionist looked over at Mama, who was sitting in a chair in the corner, looking very pale. She shrugged. 'It's Doctor Jennings or nothing.'

Safa tried to stay calm. She wanted to scream. 'We can't see a male doctor. We are Muslim women.'

But she didn't want to have to explain why a Muslim woman could not be alone with a man who wasn't her husband, brother or father. Safa was sick and tired of explaining things and translating all the time. She wanted Mama to learn English. She wanted Baba to come and help out, to be here, to be her dad and Mama's husband. She was sick of having to do everything. She was so tired, so very tired.

Safa didn't realise she was crying until a woman came up and handed her a tissue. The woman patted her on the back. 'There, there, dear. You can take my appointment with Doctor Brady and I'll go to Doctor Jennings. Doctor Brady is a female doctor.'

Safa looked up. The woman was about Mama's age and she had such kind eyes.

'Thank you so much,' Safa said, turning her back so Mama wouldn't see she was crying. 'It's so kind of you.'

'It's my pleasure. Doctor Brady is very kind and a very good doctor. Your mother will be in good hands. Don't worry, pet, it'll all be fine.'

Safa held the tissue to her mouth to stop the sob escaping. This woman's kindness was making her weep. But she had to hold it together for Mama. She took a deep breath and tried to smile. 'Thanks,' she croaked, and then dried her eyes and went back over to her mother.

When it was their turn, they shuffled into the surgery and sat opposite the doctor. Dr Brady smiled reassuringly at Safa and her mother. 'What seems to be the problem?'

Mama told Safa and Safa translated. 'Her heart is beating very fast. She fainted this morning. I made her come. She is afraid of doctors. She's afraid of being unwell. I think ...' Safa's voice shook. 'I think she's afraid of dying.'

Dr Brady reached over and patted her hand. 'You're a very responsible girl. I'm going to do everything I can to help your mum. I'm going to take your mother's blood pressure, temperature, listen to her breathing, and a few other tests. I'll explain it to you, and you can translate for her.'

They went through the tests. Dr Brady didn't say much but listened carefully to Mama's heart and lungs and took her temperature and checked her throat and her ears and her glands and measured her height and weight …

After all the tests, she told Mama to sit down. 'Has your mother been under a lot of stress lately?' she asked.

Safa almost laughed. She heard people in Ireland using the word 'stress' all the time. 'I'm so stressed about this spot on my chin', 'I'm so stressed about my hair', 'School is such a stress' … It was funny to Safa because she knew what real stress was. Mama knew what real stress was too.

'Yes, Mama has had a lot of stress.'

'I imagine you had a long and difficult journey here?' Dr Brady said gently.

Safa nodded. 'Very.'

'The good news is that your mother's vital signs are all normal. I do, however, think she is suffering from anxiety. I'm going to suggest that your mother takes some anti-anxiety medication. We can start her on a low dose and see how she tolerates it. I think it'll help her. It will help with sleep and moods and worry and should improve her quality of life.'

Mama was wary of 'foreign' doctors. She only trusted Syrian ones. But they were in Ireland now, there were no Syrian doctors, and this doctor seemed nice and knowledgeable and helpful. And if the pills helped Mama sleep and not be worried all the time, that would be a good thing.

Dr Brady, seeing her hesitate, said, 'Look, Safa, if your mum had an eye infection, I'd give her drugs to clear it up. These drugs are to help her anxiety get better. There is nothing to worry about, they are totally safe, and I am suggesting a low dose.'

Safa knew Mama wasn't sleeping. Whenever Safa woke up from one of her nightmares or had to go to the bathroom in the early morning, Safa would see Mama's light on. She'd peep in and see Mama reading or listening to the radio, trying to find the latest news from home.

Safa gently explained to Mama that the doctor was giving her pills to help with stress and sleep. She said they would make her calmer so that her heart wouldn't beat too fast and she wouldn't faint.

Mama didn't argue; she was clearly happy to take something to help her. She nodded and took the prescription. As they were about to leave, Dr Brady stopped them.

'Safa, I'd like to talk to you about how you are feeling,' she said.

'I'm fine,' Safa lied.

'I'm not sure you are, pet. You have a lot of responsibility on your shoulders for a young girl. How are you coping with it all? Are you sleeping? Do you have nightmares? How is your anxiety?'

Safa swallowed the lump in her throat. Every time she thought about the fact that they hadn't heard from Baba in almost ten days, she wanted to scream, but she didn't want to fall apart in front of Mama. 'I'm OK, thank you. I started in Saint Mary's school a few weeks ago and it's good. I like the girls and I'm doing well in my schoolwork.'

Dr Brady smiled. 'I'm delighted to hear that – it's a good school. But I imagine you have been through a lot and it's not easy to deal with it all. Are you sleeping? You look tired.'

Safa didn't want to talk about her nightmares. She wanted to forget about them. Besides, Mama was staring at her, trying to understand what the doctor was asking her.

'Why can't we go now?' Mama asked. 'What is she asking you? I want to get the medicine and go home now, Safa.'

Safa squeezed her mother's hand. 'I'm fine, thank you, Doctor. I'm just worried about Mama. We need to go now. She needs some rest.'

'All right, but remember, my door is always open to you, Safa. I'll leave a note at reception so they know that if you come in, I'll see you straight away.'

'Thank you for being so kind,' Safa said.

Dr Brady smiled a sad smile and patted her on the shoulder. 'Your mum is lucky to have such a caring daughter.'

Mama held Safa's hand as they walked out.

They went to the pharmacy next door to get the pills and then walked slowly home. Safa gave Mama one of the pills and a glass of water and then helped her into bed.

'I love you, Habibti,' Mama said, holding Safa's face in her hands. 'You are my angel, my life. I thank Allah every day for sending you to me.'

'I love you too, Mama.' Safa smiled.

'I'm sorry I gave you a fright this morning. I'm just tired. Don't worry about me – I am strong. I come from a long line of strong women. I will always be here for you, Safa. I will always look after you.' Mama kissed Safa's cheeks and then lay back on the pillow and was asleep within seconds.

Safa wanted to believe her, but she knew that nothing in life was certain. No one could promise to be there for you for ever, because you didn't know what was around the corner. She had been so happy in Syria but then the war happened, and everything changed and was horrible, and now Baba was far away and Mama was not well.

Safa went down to do her homework. They had an English essay to write. The title was 'My Favourite Animal'.

Safa thought of Adira's sweet furry face. She put her head in her hands and cried.

CHAPTER NINE

Ruby

ate that night, Ruby was lying on her bed, watching *The Wizard of Oz* for the zillionth time. She wanted so badly to play Dorothy. The auditions were on Monday and she knew Amber had been practising 'Somewhere Over the Rainbow' all week. She knew that Amber was her main competition for the lead role.

Ruby paused the video. She had to prepare herself for the worst. She might not get Dorothy. If she didn't, she wanted to be the Scarecrow. He was the second-best part, in her opinion. The character description said, 'Though the scarecrow's dearest wish is that Oz give him a brain, he is already possessed of intelligence. He learns quickly and usually comes up with a helpful idea when the characters face challenges.'

Ruby could see herself as Dorothy, starring in the show as parents and the other students gasped at how incredible she was. 'She'll win an Oscar some day,' they'd say.

Ruby stood up in front of the mirror and took a bow. 'Thank you,' she said to her imaginary audience.

'What are you doing, you freak?'

Ruby spun around. Orla was behind her. Dammit, she hadn't heard her sister coming in. 'Nothing.'

Orla rolled her eyes and threw herself onto her bed.

Ruby looked at the clock. It was midnight. Orla was supposed to have been home by ten thirty. 'Did Mum see you come in?'

Orla snorted. 'Are you joking? She's fast asleep on the couch.'

Ruby sniffed; her sister smelt funny. She smelt like Dad's beers. 'Oh my God, have you been drinking?'

'No.'

'Yes you have. You stink.'

'Shut up, you idiot.'

'Mum and Dad will go mental if they find out.'

Orla's eyes narrowed. 'How would they find out? You're not going to tell them, now, are you?' She grabbed Ruby's arm and pulled it behind her back.

'Ouch, you're hurting me.'

'Swear you won't say anything!'

'I swear.'

Orla let go of Ruby's arm. Ruby rubbed it where it ached. 'You shouldn't be drinking, though. You know it's wrong. You're only fifteen.'

'I'll be sixteen next month, not that anyone in this house will remember.'

Ruby's mind flashed back to last year, when everyone had forgotten Orla's fifteenth birthday because Robbie was in hospital. Mum had remembered two days after and felt so bad. She'd kept apologising to Orla, who had pretended she didn't care, but Ruby knew she did. Mum had tried to make it up to her by buying her a silver necklace with her name on it, but Orla had only worn it once. Ruby knew her sister thought it was dorky.

'Don't do it again, Orla, seriously. Mum and Dad don't need to worry about you drinking. It's not fair. They've enough to be worried about.'

Orla kicked off her boots and lay back on her bed. 'Mum and Dad wouldn't notice if I had vodka for breakfast. They're too wrapped up in Robbie and all his drama to notice whether I'm alive or dead.'

'That's not fair! They do try.'

Orla sat up. 'That's a load of crap and you know it. Since he came along they never take us out, we never do anything as a family, we never have fun, they're permanently exhausted and pretty much forget we exist. It's all about Robbie. I wish he'd never been born.'

Ruby waved her arms. 'Don't say that – take it back. It's mean and wrong and ... and ... and ...'

'And true,' Orla said.

'No, no, it isn't!' Ruby shouted. She had to push back the words. It was wrong. Orla shouldn't say things like that. But deep down, although she would never ever admit it, Ruby sometimes felt the same.

The door snapped open and Mum came in. 'For God's sake, Ruby, be quiet. You'll wake Robbie up. It took me nearly two hours to get him to sleep,' she hissed. 'You should be asleep. What are you doing up at this hour?' Mum took the iPad from Ruby's bed and turned to leave the room. Turning to Orla, she asked, 'What time did you get in at?'

'About twenty past ten. You were with Robbie, so I didn't go in to you.'

'Good girl. OK, goodnight, girls.'

Mum left the room and Orla turned to Ruby. 'See? She doesn't even notice if I'm here or not.'

Ruby cuddled up under her duvet and turned out her bedside lamp. She said a prayer that Dad would have a good night taxi driving, that Mum and Robbie would sleep well and that Orla wouldn't drink again.

The weekend went too quickly, as always. Monday morning came and when Ruby went down for breakfast Mum was up making her lunch.

'Hello, pet. I've made you salami sandwiches. I'm afraid the bread isn't very fresh, but I cut the crusts off so it's not too bad. I'm sorry I never made it to the supermarket yesterday. Every time I tried to leave Robbie kicked off. I'll go today.'

'It's OK, Mum, the bread looks fine.' Ruby poured

cornflakes into her bowl. 'Actually, Mum, I just wanted to remind you that it's Orla's birthday next month. I think we should all make a fuss because of last year.'

Mum's hand flew to her mouth. 'Oh God, I still feel sick about forgetting it last year. I'll put a reminder into my phone now, so I get her present good and early. Thanks for reminding me, Ruby. You're such a good sister and daughter. I don't tell you enough.'

Mum came over and put her arms around Ruby from behind and kissed her on the head. It was nice. Like, really, really nice. 'So, what's going on with you?'

'We have the auditions for the musical today.'

'Oh good luck! I hope you get a good part. I'm so sorry we missed you last year. God, all I seem to do is apologise to you girls these days. I'm a rubbish mother to you both.'

Ruby turned around. Mum looked so sad. She stood up and hugged her. 'No you're not – you're just tied up a lot with Robbie.'

'I know, but it's not fair on you and Orla. I'm sorry, pet, I really am. I'll try to do better. I keep thinking Robbie will get easier as he gets older, less needy of me, but it seems to be the opposite.'

Ruby didn't know what to say so she just patted her mum on the back and said, 'It's OK,' over and over.

Orla came in and went over to the cupboard. She pulled out a Weetabix box and shook it. 'It's empty.'

'There's cornflakes here on the table,' Mum said.

'I don't want cornflakes. I want Weetabix.'

'I'll get to the shops today.'

'That's what you said on Saturday and Sunday.'

'Leave Mum alone,' Ruby snapped. 'You could have gone to the shop yourself.'

'When?' Orla shouted. 'I was working in the café all day Saturday and Sunday. Remember, I have a job where I work to earn my own money, so I don't have to ask Mum and Dad for anything, because I know that every single penny Dad earns goes into getting Robbie to say three bloody words.'

Ruby gripped Orla's arm. She had to get her sister to stop. Mum didn't need any more guilt piled on top of her. 'Stop it. Mum's doing her best.'

'So am I,' Orla hissed.

The door opened and Dad wheeled Robbie in. 'Look who's awake and up and dressed.'

'Hi, sweetheart,' Mum said, kissing Robbie on the cheek. Turning to Dad, she said, 'Thanks for getting him up. You can get some rest now.'

'Great, wake me up at one.'

'OK, will do.'

'Have a good day in school, girls. Try smiling, Orla – it'll make people like you more.' He winked at his older daughter and left to get some rest.

'Hi hi hi!' Robbie said, waving at them.

'Hi, Robbie.' Ruby went over and hugged him.

'Hi Robbie.' Orla waved back. 'OK, well, seeing as there is nothing I want to eat, I'll head in early.' Orla put her backpack on her shoulder and walked towards the door.

'Bye, pet, I'll get the Weetabix today,' Mum said.

'Bye bye, I dove you!' Robbie shouted.

Orla turned and looked down at her little brother's smiling face. He was wearing a light blue jumper that matched his eyes and his blond hair was sticking up at the back. He beamed up at his sister. Orla paused and then, half smiling, whispered, 'I love you too, even though you drive me nuts. Bye bye, Robbie.'

When Ruby turned back, there were tears in Mum's eyes. 'She does love him. She really does,' Mum said, smiling through her happy tears.

CHAPTER TEN

Safa

S afa crossed her fingers under her desk. Mr Parson
was about to read out the parts for *The Wizard of
Oz* and Safa could feel Ruby shaking beside her.

She reached over and squeezed her friend's hand.
'Good luck,' she whispered.

Ruby nodded, too nervous to reply.

'Dorothy will be played by Amber. Congratulations.'
Mr Parson smiled over at Amber, who was grinning
from ear to ear.

Ruby's shoulders drooped. Safa felt really bad for her friend.

'The Lion will be played by Dervla, the Tin Man by Chrissie.'

Ruby shrank down in her chair. *Please let her get the Scarecrow*, Safa prayed.

'And the Scarecrow will be played by Ruby.'

'Yes!' Safa didn't realise she'd said it out loud.

Ruby grinned at her. 'Thanks.'

'I'm so happy for you. Obviously, I think you should be Dorothy but the Scarecrow is a much more interesting character.'

'I'm happy enough,' Ruby said. 'I was worried I wasn't going to get anything. It's a pity Amber and Chrissie are two of the other main parts. They're such cows.'

'Just ignore them,' Clara said, turning around in her chair to face them.

'Clara,' Ruby replied, 'any chance you can help me with my lines after school?'

Clara shook her head. 'Sorry, I have violin practice.'

Ruby rolled her eyes. 'Denise?'

'No can do, I have to go to my brother's football final.'

Safa was a bit hurt that Ruby hadn't asked her. She decided to offer to help. 'I can help you if you like,' she said.

Ruby turned to look at her. 'Really? Would you?'

'Of course, I'd be happy to.'

'Thanks. But –' Ruby paused. 'We'd have to go back to my house because Mum has a dental appointment. Maybe we can do it tomorrow. I can go back to your house.'

'No, today is good. I have football practice after school tomorrow. I'll text my mum and tell her I'll be late home.'

Safa waited until breaktime and sent her mother a text telling her she was going to a friend's house after school and not to worry. She gave her Ruby's address, so her mother wouldn't start worrying, and promised she'd be home in time for dinner.

Her mother texted back that she was to be home by six sharp and that she was to call her when she got to Ruby's house, so she knew she was safe.

Safa sighed. Mama suffocated her a bit. She was

constantly worried something bad was going to happen. Safa knew it was because so many bad things *had* happened, but she also needed to be allowed to breathe.

⬧

After school Safa walked home with Ruby. Her friend seemed nervous and kept fiddling with the strap on her backpack.

When they got to the end of Ruby's road, which was only two streets over from where Safa lived, Ruby stopped. 'Look, my little brother Robbie has learning disabilities. Suzie, the speech therapist, will be there now so we won't have to go in to him, but he can be kind of loud and shout and freak out sometimes. It's not his fault; he was born that way. Just ignore it. We'll go straight up to my room. OK?'

Safa nodded.

When they got to the house, Ruby opened the front door and bumped into her mother.

'Hi,' said Ruby. 'I thought you were going to the dentist?'

Her mother had her face in her handbag, looking for something. 'I am – I'm late because Robbie went mad when he saw Suzie today. I don't know why – he usually likes her.' She pulled keys from her bag. 'There they are – I have to dash.'

'Hello, Mrs Fitzpatrick, it's very nice to meet you.' Safa put her hand out as her father had taught her.

Fiona looked up. 'Oh hello – I'm sorry – I didn't even see you there. Very nice to meet you too.' Ruby's mother reminded Safa a bit of Mama. You could see she was a pretty woman, but life had created lines and dark circles under her eyes. She looked exhausted and very thin.

'This is Safa; she's from Syria,' said Ruby.

'Welcome to Ireland,' Fiona said, speaking slowly and loudly.

'Oh for God's sake, Mum, her English is better than mine.' Ruby's face was red.

'Oh right, sorry! I've got to go. My tooth is killing me. Bye.'

Ruby's mother dashed out the door with her coat half on.

'What's for dinner?' Ruby called.

Her mother turned around. 'Sorry, we went to the

shops, but Robbie saw a big dog and went crazy, so we had to come home. Check the freezer, there might be something in there. Your dad started work early, so you're on your own. Sorry, love, I have to go, I'm late already. Nice to meet you,' Fiona waved at Safa.

'Great,' Ruby muttered under her breath. 'I'm starving and there's no dinner.'

They went into the kitchen, where Ruby rummaged around in the cupboards, fridge and freezer to find something to eat.

The countertop was covered in papers, letters, medicine bottles, pens, receipts and other random items like earplugs and a teddy bear. There were three half-drunk cups of coffee on the kitchen table. Safa thought of her kitchen at home, where Mama had everything tidied away and the countertop was always so clean and there was always freshly cooked food to eat. She felt bad for Ruby.

Ruby turned to Safa. 'Well, I guess we'll just have to eat these for now.' She held up two cereal bars. 'I don't like them, but Robbie does so we always have loads of them. Whatever Robbie likes, Mum remembers to buy,' she grumbled. 'Tea?'

'Do you have any green tea?'

Ruby laughed. 'We barely have anything. It's normal tea or nothing.'

Safa smiled. 'Sure, normal tea is fine.'

The door opened. Orla threw her bag on the floor. 'Don't talk to me. I've had a crappy day.' She went over to the cupboard. Her skirt was hitched right up like a miniskirt. Safa didn't know how she wasn't freezing. Her legs were very brown in some parts but had streaks of white on the sides. Her hair was up in a very high ponytail and she had spidery eyelashes on.

'Are you kidding me?' Orla groaned when she saw the empty cupboard. 'She promised she'd go shopping today.'

Ruby handed Safa a cup of tea. 'Mum said she tried but Robbie kicked off, so she had to come home.'

'I'm sick of this,' Orla said. 'Here, make me a cup of tea.'

'Please?'

'Just do it, Ruby.'

'Fine.'

Safa had always thought it would be lovely to have an older sister, but now she wasn't so sure.

Orla picked at the red nail polish on her thumb. 'I got a week of early morning detention from Mrs Oliver.'

'What did you do?' Ruby handed her sister a cup of tea.

'I shoved Caroline Keeley up against a wall and told her she was an ugly cow who would die alone.'

Ruby giggled. 'Seriously?'

Orla took a sip of her tea. 'Yep.'

'Why?'

'Because she is,' Orla said, 'and also because she said Conor Levy wouldn't go out with me because my brother is a retard.'

'What?!' Ruby slammed down her cup of tea, spilling some of it on the table. 'How dare she?'

'Did you tell Mrs Oliver what Caroline said to you?' Safa asked. Surely if Orla's headmistress knew what a horrible thing Caroline had said, she would have understood Orla's actions.

Orla rolled her eyes. 'Caroline Keeley's dad paid for the new tennis court. Mrs Oliver doesn't care what that cow said about Robbie.'

'But that's not fair – she was cruel about your brother,' Safa said.

Orla snorted, 'Fair? Since when has life ever been fair? I mean you're a refugee, for God's sake – how can you possibly think life is fair?'

Safa frowned. 'Because if we stop believing it, then we lose hope.'

Orla looked at her. 'You talk like someone way older. But seriously, you need to let go of the fair thing. It'll just melt your head. Is it fair that Robbie is the way he is? No. Is it fair that you had to leave your warm country and come and live in the rain in Ireland? No. Is it fair that I'm gorgeous and Ruby isn't? No.'

'Thanks a lot,' Ruby said.

'I'm only messing.' Orla grinned. 'You're not ugly, you just need a lot of work.'

They heard a roar.

'Uh oh, someone's not happy,' Orla sighed.

'NO NO NO NO!' a boy's voice roared.

'You better go in, Ruby,' Orla said. 'He obviously doesn't want Suzie's speech therapy class today.'

'No way, I have a friend over. You go in.'

'You're better with him.'

'No,' Ruby hissed.

Safa stood up. 'I'll go.'

Orla and Ruby grabbed her and pulled her back. 'No way,' they both said.

'He does not react well to new people,' Ruby explained.

'I'd like to meet him.'

'Why?' Orla asked.

'Because he's your brother,' Safa said simply.

'Yeah but … but Robbie is not like other brothers,' Ruby explained.

'I know that, but I'd still like to meet him. Could I come in with you? Would that be OK?'

'NO NO NO NO!' Robbie roared.

The kitchen door opened, and Suzie's head appeared. 'Sorry, girls, any chance you could come in and talk to Robbie? He's very off form today.'

Ruby and Orla both stood up. Safa followed them into the lounge. There in the corner of the room, in a wheelchair, was a blond, blue-eyed child shouting at the top of his voice. Orla and Ruby rushed over to calm him down. But he was kicking his legs and waving his arms and his shouting just kept getting louder.

Safa's mind went back to that awful night on the overcrowded rubber dinghy in the middle of the ocean trying to get from Turkey to Greece. She could hear the woman's voice in her head, screaming, 'We're all going to die!' Over and over. They all tried to talk to her to calm the woman down, but it was only when the old lady sang that she stopped.

Safa opened her mouth and began to sing. It was a well-known Syrian lullaby, the same one the old lady had sung to calm the frightened woman on that dark night. Safa closed her eyes and sang it for Robbie, for Ruby, for Orla, for Mama and Baba and everyone whose life was not fair.

Safa lost herself in the song. She could no longer hear Robbie shouting. She was no longer in this house in Ireland. She was far away, feeling the sun on her back as she ran up the path to her grandparents' house. She was young and free and happy.

When she finished the song, she opened her eyes. Complete silence. Four pairs of eyes were staring at her, and four mouths were open.

'Who is this magician and can she come every week?' Suzie beamed at her.

'Oh my God, that was incredible,' Orla said.

'Safa!' Ruby gasped. 'You can sing. That was … like magic.'

A shout came from the corner. 'AGAIN!' Robbie said, beaming at her.

CHAPTER ELEVEN

Ruby

Ruby looked out at the rain pouring down outside. Miss Ingle was droning on about photosynthesis, which was so boring.

She peeped over at Safa, presuming she'd be leaning forward taking notes, but she wasn't. She was looking out of the window. She looked sad. Like, really sad, deep-down sad.

Ruby scribbled down a note and passed it to Safa.

Safa scribbled a reply and passed it back. 'I'm sad

because it's my dad's birthday. He's forty-two today and we haven't heard from him in a while.'

Ruby's heart sank. Poor Safa. She had to do something.

At breaktime, while Safa went to the bathroom, Ruby pulled Clara and Denise aside. 'We have to help Safa. It's her dad's birthday and she's gutted.'

'Did you talk to your mum?' Denise asked Clara.

'Yeah, but she's all stressed about some big, huge case she's working on and she's hardly ever home, so I didn't ask her to help us, I just pretended I was curious for no particular reason. Anyway, Mum said it's the Minister for Justice who makes the decisions about refugees and their families.'

'OK, so how do we find the Minister?' Ruby asked.

'I Googled it. The Minister is a man and his name is Gary O'Gorman and he is really old and bald, and he looks a bit scary, but he is the person who makes the decisions so we need to write to him.'

'Like an email?' Denise asked.

'No, I think we need to write an actual letter,' Clara said.

'Like in the old days?' Ruby asked.

'Yeah.'

'Should we buy a card and write him a card? We could get one of those adorable ones with a kitten or a puppy on it and then beg him to let Safa's dad come to Ireland and he'd never be able to say no to that,' Ruby suggested.

Clara bit her thumbnail. 'He's a politician, Ruby, not a kid. He doesn't care about cute kitten cards.'

Ruby bristled. 'OK, then, what do you want to write it on?'

'I could get some of my mum's fancy work notepaper. She has this thick cream paper with her law firm's name on the top.'

Ruby thought that did sound good, very professional. But she still thought the kitten was a good idea. It would soften him up when he saw the cuteness of it.

'OMG!' Denise clapped her hands. 'Why don't we pretend we're lawyers writing to him from your mum's company? That way he'll take us seriously.'

'Brilliant!' Ruby was impressed with her friend's thinking. This was perfect. If the old minister thought they were actual real-life lawyers then he'd definitely let Safa's dad come to Ireland.

Clara put her hands up. 'Hang on a second. That could be illegal.'

'Yeah, but we're not actually saying we're lawyers, we're just using the paper,' Denise said. Denise was really good at bending rules. It came from having four older brothers who constantly bent and broke them.

'I suppose so, but –'

Ruby interrupted Clara before she started backing down from the plan. 'It's perfect, Clara. Just get the paper ASAP and we'll think about what to say.'

'I think Clara should write it 'cause she's, like, the cleverest,' Denise said. 'No offence, Ruby.'

Ruby grinned. 'I'm not mental. I know she's way smarter than me.'

'Shouldn't we tell Safa?' Clara asked.

'No.' Ruby was firm about this. 'It mightn't work and then she'll have got her hopes up for nothing.'

Ruby knew all about getting your hopes up. Mum and Dad got their hopes up all the time when Robbie was little. They kept saying, 'Maybe he's not really brain damaged. Maybe he will walk and talk and have a normal life. Maybe he'll be able to be independent. Maybe he'll be able to feed himself …' But then things just got worse.

Ruby would not let Safa get her hopes up. It was cruel. You should only tell someone good news when it actually happened and not give them false hope.

'OK, so what should I say in the letter? Let's just scribble down some notes.' Clara took out a copybook and pen.

'Dear Sir,' Denise said.

'Please can you help our friend Safa find her dad who is stuck in Greece?' Ruby added.

Clara shook her head. 'No, it has to be way more fancy. Like, "Dear Sir, we are very sorry to disturb you as we know that you are a very busy man making lots of important decisions and helping to run the country with Justice. We would like to inform you of a very serious issue that has come to our attention."'

'That's good,' Denise said. 'It sounds really professional.'

'"Our best friend Safa, who is a refugee from the war-torn country of Syria, which borders Turkey and Iran" –'

'Hold on, I don't think you need to tell him that. I mean, he'd know all about geography already. He must have done super well in his exams if he is a big minister now,' Ruby pointed out.

Clara shrugged. 'Fine, I was just trying to show him that we know about Syria.'

Ruby bit her tongue. Clara was always trying to show how much she knew, but for goodness' sake, the really old minister didn't need a geography lesson.

'"…from the war-torn country of Syria, is living in Ireland with her mother but her father is – " No.' Clara scribbled that line out. '"Her family is torn apart because her father is being held up in Greece. We are begging" – No – "We are pleading with you to find a way to bring Safa's beloved father to Ireland so this family can be together again."'

'Wow!' Denise was impressed. 'Brilliant letter, Clara.'

'It is really good,' Ruby agreed. 'Maybe we could add in something about Safa being a brilliant student and telling everyone that education is freedom. I think he'd like that.'

Clara tapped her pen against her teeth. 'Maybe, but I don't want to make it too long either. The man is very busy.'

Ruby wasn't backing down, and she knew Clara was a tiny bit jealous of the fact that Safa was getting better marks than her in some of the weekly tests. 'We need to put that in the letter.'

'Fine. "Safa is already doing well in school and believes that education is freedom. Her father is a teacher and Ireland needs more good teachers."'

'I think you should put in something about her being a really good goalie too,' Denise said.

Clara wasn't having any of it. 'For goodness' sake, Denise, this is a government minister – he doesn't care about goalies.'

'Keep your hair on. Jeez.'

Clara bit her nail. 'Yes, well, I'm a bit stressed. I'm doing a lot of the work here.'

'OK, fine, if Safa's dad gets out, you can take the credit,' Denise said.

Ruby frowned. Hang on, this was her idea. She was the one who came up with the plan. There was no way Clara was getting all the praise.

'I'll write it up tonight,' Clara said. 'Mum's up in Dublin for the night and my minder doesn't care what I do as long as I don't interrupt her when she's watching her TV programmes. Mum keeps a stash of the notepaper in her desk at home. I'll use her fancy ink pen so it looks really official.'

'Brilliant. Bring it in tomorrow so we can all sign it,' Ruby said.

'OK, but are we using our real names?' Clara asked.

'I am,' Ruby said.

'Me too,' Denise said.

'OK. Then me too,' Clara said. 'And I'll write my mobile number underneath, so they call me and not Mum.'

'You're so lucky you have a phone. I can't wait to get mine,' Denise said.

Ruby didn't think Clara was that lucky to have a phone. She'd had one since she was six. It was because her mum was always working. It was Mimi, her childminder, who picked her up from school and cooked her dinner. The phone was the main way Clara communicated with her mother. They didn't spend much time together at all, except on Sundays, which were supposed to be their 'bonding days', but Clara said her mum often took her into the office while she worked and Clara sat on the couch in the corner of her mum's office and read books.

Ruby didn't know which was better or worse: a mum who was physically there but a dad in Greece, a lawyer mum who was always working and no dad, a mum and dad who were permanently exhausted and distracted by Robbie and never remembered anything, or a mum like Denise's mum, who roared and shouted all the time because the four boys drove her nuts.

Maybe there was no better. Maybe you just had to make the best of what you had.

CHAPTER TWELVE

Safa

Safa sat on Orla's bed, opposite Ruby, who was sitting on her own bed, trying to recite lines from *The Wizard of Oz*.

'Come on, you can do it,' said Safa.

Ruby closed her eyes and thought hard. 'Some people without brains do an awful lot of talking, don't they?'

'Yes! Well done,' Safa said. 'You know all your lines now.'

'Thanks to you,' Ruby said.

Safa had been helping Ruby a lot over the past few weeks. It was nice. She liked being able to help people. She'd done it in the camp, helping to translate for other refugees with no English. After that first day when she met Robbie and calmed him down by singing, Ruby was happy to bring Safa to her house. In fact, over the past three weeks, Safa had been in Ruby's house about six times. Safa had invited Ruby to come back to her house, but Ruby always had to go home to help with Robbie.

Robbie liked Safa. He smiled when she came in and waved his arms when he saw her. She had to sing the song for him every time, which was a bit annoying, but she didn't really mind. It always made him smile and he looked so cute when he smiled.

Orla barged into the room. 'Shift,' she ordered Safa.

Safa got up and moved over to Ruby's bed.

'OK, nerds, I need you to help make me look drop-dead gorgeous. I'm going to a party in Lorraine Kenny's and Conor Levy is going to be there and this is the night when he's going to fall head over heels for me. I need to look super-hot. Like, hotter than hot. The hottest person ever.'

'OK, we get it,' Ruby groaned.

'How can we help?' Safa asked.

'Well, I need fake tan on my back and shoulders 'cause I want to wear a strappy top, and I need my nails done too. I also need you to wave the back of my hair. I can do the front but the back needs to be perfect too.'

Ruby shook her head. 'No way. I am not curling your hair. Last time you made me do it I burnt my fingers on the wand.'

Orla rolled her eyes. 'That's because you're an idiot. Anyway, Safa can do that and you can do my tan.' She bent down to plug in her curling wand.

'Why do you put all that tan on your body?' Safa asked. 'You have lovely smooth white skin; why do you cover it up with all that fake tan? And those crazy fake eyelashes that look like spiders?'

Orla looked at her as if she was mad. 'Lovely white skin? It's horrible pasty skin with freckles, urgh. At least with tan on you look better: thinner, healthier and hotter. And false lashes make your eyes look way bigger and nicer. Your eyes could do with some make-up. They'd look much better.'

'But you don't look better with all the stuff you wear. You look ... well ... a bit orange and silly.'

Ruby covered her mouth to stop a giggle escaping.

'Silly? Silly would be going out with pasty white legs in a minidress. I'd scare boys away. Silly would be going out without my lashes on and small piggy eyes. Silly would be not making myself look better.'

'Yes, but wouldn't a little bit of make-up be better than so much that you can barely see your eyes or skin?'

Orla sighed. 'You don't get it because you have lovely skin and your eyes are quite big. You wake up looking OK. I wake up looking like crap. Pasty, small eyes and freckles. If I didn't wear make-up, no boy would go near me. I need it. When I'm all made up I feel hot and it gives me confidence.'

Safa thought about that. If all the make-up made Orla feel stronger and more confident, then it was a good thing. But Safa still thought she would look much better without it.

An hour later, Orla came out of the bathroom and twirled. She was wearing a tight silver top with tiny straps, a very short black skirt and high-heeled sandals.

Safa looked out the bedroom window. It was pelting down with rain. How did Irish girls go out with so few clothes on in a cold, wet country? Did they not feel the cold? Were they just used to it? Did they not mind having wet toes?

'Girls, dinner!' Ruby's mum called.

Safa had told Mama that she was going to stay at Ruby's till about nine. Mama had got to know Ruby a bit in the yard at pick-up time, and she was happy that Safa had a friend, so she didn't mind.

Orla put a long skirt over her mini and zipped up a jacket over her top. Then from her rucksack she pulled out a small bottle of beer. She opened the top and took a long drink.

'Oh my God, Orla, Mum and Dad will go mad if they find out you're drinking.' Ruby's eyes were wide.

'Oh relax. You're such a bore. Everyone drinks.'

'No they don't,' Ruby said.

'OK, well, lots of people do. It's fun. I want to get a little buzzed up before I see Conor. You better not tell – I'll kill you if you do.' Orla hid the bottle inside her jacket.

'As if I'm going to upset Mum and Dad with your drinking,' Ruby snapped.

Safa didn't understand the drinking either. Why did Irish teenagers drink? She was often awake at night after her nightmares and she'd seen some of the teenagers who lived in her estate coming home, stumbling in their gardens, trying to get their keys out of their bags, vomiting into hedges, falling down ... Safa thought it was dangerous. She'd seen people in the camps drinking. It was usually young men and it always led to trouble. Fights broke out when the men drank too much. Harsh words were said, and bones were broken. Baba said alcohol was bad for you. He said it caused many problems in families. He said everyone should stay away from it. Safa was worried about Orla drinking. She hoped she didn't get into trouble.

They all headed downstairs. Safa whispered to Ruby, 'Maybe you should tell your parents about Orla drinking.'

Ruby stopped dead on the stairs. 'Are you mad? My parents are stressed out all the time over Robbie. The last thing they need is to worry about Orla.'

'But what if she drinks too much?'

'Then she'll learn not to do it again,' Ruby said, and continued down the stairs.

Fiona looked up as they came in. 'You look very dressed up, love,' she said to Orla.

'I'm going out, Mum, remember I told you? A party at Lorraine's.'

'Oh yes, sorry, it slipped my mind. Well, you'd better have some dinner before you go.'

'No, I'm good, there'll be food there,' Orla said.

'Oh, all right, are you sure?'

'Yep.'

'I like that long skirt on you. It's much nicer than those miniskirts you wear.'

'Yeah, me too.' Orla winked at Safa. 'OK, see you later.'

'Be home before eleven-thirty,' Fiona told Orla as her eldest daughter rushed out the front door.

Orla waved and slammed the door behind her.

'Now, it's pork chops and mash tonight,' Fiona said.

'Muuuuuuuum,' Ruby groaned.

'What? You like pork!'

'I know, but Safa can't eat it, remember? She's Muslim.'

'Oh Safa, pet, I'm so sorry. I'm such an idiot. I didn't think.'

Safa felt sorry for Fiona. She always seemed so stressed out. 'It's fine, honestly. I'm happy to eat the mashed potatoes and peas.'

Fiona went over to the fridge. 'I have some ham – Oh no, that's pork too. Rashers, pork … God, I actually have no meat that isn't pork.'

'Please don't worry.' Safa tried to reassure her.

The woman was almost in tears. 'I'm sorry,' Fiona said. 'And you are so good to come and help Ruby with her lines. Maybe I could –'

'MMMMMMMMMMM!' Robbie banged his juice cup down on the tray attached to his wheelchair.

'More juice, Robbie?' Fiona asked.

'MMMMMMMMMMM!' he wailed.

Fiona rushed over to refill his cup. But it wasn't what he wanted. Robbie flung his cup across the room.

'Oh dear, he's been off-form all day.' Fiona picked up the cup and the top that had come off and then proceeded to wipe up the juice that was now all over the kitchen floor.

'He's been off-form all week,' Ruby muttered.

'MMMMMMMMM!'

Safa looked around. There was a carton of milk on the countertop. Robbie seemed to be looking in that direction, but it was hard to tell because his eyes were darting about.

She got up and held up the milk. 'Milk, Robbie?'

'Es,' he smiled.

Safa had got very good at guessing what people wanted in the camp in Greece. There were people there from all over the world speaking many languages and it was difficult to communicate. But Safa had learned to read people's minds. Not like an actual mind reader or anything, but she had learned to observe and translate movement and gestures as well as words.

'Oh, you clever girl.' Fiona poured milk into Robbie's cup and put the lid firmly on. 'You really are a gem.' She handed the cup to Robbie, who sucked noisily. 'How are things going with you and your mum? Is she still going to her English lessons?'

'Yes, she's going more regularly now, which is great. It's hard for her but she's definitely getting better. Sometimes she has bad days and she doesn't want to go, but mostly she goes.'

Fiona ran her hand through Robbie's soft, blond curls. 'We all have bad days, but as long as the good ones outweigh the bad ones, we'll be OK.'

'My father always says we have to look at the glass as half full – it's the only way to have a happy life. Always look for the silver lining. But sometimes it's hard, isn't it?'

Fiona nodded; her eyes filled with tears. 'Yes it is, pet. It certainly is.'

Robbie shouted 'Again!' at Safa.

'No, she's not singing to him again. It's not fair,' Ruby said.

'AGAIN!' Robbie roared, his face going red.

'Not now, Robbie, Safa is having her dinner,' Fiona said gently.

'AGAIN!' He began to shake.

'Stop him, Mum, it's not OK. I can't invite Safa over any more if he's going to do this every time. It's embarrassing. It puts her on the spot all the time.' Ruby was in tears.

Fiona looked at Safa with pleading eyes. They reminded Safa of the eyes of a refugee from Somalia who was begging the Red Cross for medicine for her sick child. Or the eyes of a young man she'd seen pleading with the Greek authorities not to send him back to Iran. Or the eyes of her father when he told her she had to go to Ireland with Mama without him. 'I'll follow you,' he'd promised, but where was he now?

'It's OK, Ruby, I like singing,' Safa lied. She didn't like singing that much at all, but she wanted to help Fiona, and Ruby and Robbie. And maybe if she did good things for other people, then good things would happen to her and she'd hear from Baba soon.

So she opened her mouth and sang …

CHAPTER THIRTEEN

Ruby

That evening, Ruby was going over her lines when she heard a bang on the window.

Safa jumped off the bed. 'What's that?' she said.

Ruby went over to her bedroom window and pulled back the curtains. Orla was outside. She'd climbed up onto the garage roof and was leaning over, thumping on the window.

Ruby opened the window and her sister fell in, head first, and landed with a thump on the floor.

She was soaking from the rain and she just lay in a ball on the floor.

Safa went over to her and crouched down beside her. 'Orla, Orla, are you all right?'

Orla began to sob.

Oh my God, Ruby thought, Orla hardly ever cried. She was so strong. She was by miles the strongest person in the family. Ruby was shocked. She didn't know what to do.

Safa tried to pull Orla up. 'You need to get out of those wet clothes, or you'll get a cold.'

Orla staggered to her feet. Her mascara was streaked in two black lines down her cheeks. Her lipstick was smudged and her hair was all straggly and wet.

'What happened?' Ruby asked. 'Why are you home so early?' It was only nine o'clock and Orla was allowed out until eleven-thirty.

'I had – oh God.' Orla put her hand over her mouth and ran to the bin in the corner of the bedroom. She proceeded to vomit. Safa went over and held her hair back.

Ruby held her nose. Gross. What the hell was wrong with Orla?

Safa rubbed Orla's back and waited for her to finish.

Orla turned around and wiped her mouth with her hand. She plonked down on her bed.

'Are you OK?' Ruby asked.

'I'm drunk,' Orla said, slurring her words.

'What? Are you mad? Mum and Dad will go mental if they find out and you'll be grounded for life.'

'I don't care,' Orla said, as tears ran down her cheeks. 'I never want to go out again anyway.'

'What happened at the party?' Safa asked.

Orla turned to look at her. 'I'll tell you exactly what happened. I was chatting to Conor Levy, the best-looking boy there by miles, and he was definitely keen, and then I went to the loo. When I came back, I heard Kylie Phelan telling him that my brother was a retard and there were retard genes in my family. She said we were all a bit "mental" and he should stay away from me. And then … and then …' Orla began to sob. 'She … she kissed him and he kissed her back. I hate him and I hate her. I hope she gets run over by a car on her way home and dies a slow and painful death.'

Safa patted her back.

Ruby stood up and kicked the leg of her bed. 'OMG, what a cow. How dare she say that about Robbie?' Anger pulsed through her veins. 'How dare she say that about our family? Robbie was just really unlucky, it could happen to anyone. I hate her too.' Ruby felt tears prick her own eyes.

She was sick of people judging their family because of Robbie. Before he was born they were just 'the Fitzpatricks'. But now they were 'those poor Fitzpatricks with the special-needs kid'. She hated it with all her heart. She didn't want people to pity them. They were fine. Well, OK, they weren't really, but they were getting on with things. They were a family. They loved each other and what family was perfect anyway?

Safa fished about in her backpack and handed each sister a tissue. Safa always seemed to know what to do. Ruby wondered how she did it. Was it because she was a refugee? Did refugees always have things you might need in their backpacks?

Orla lay back on the bed and groaned. 'God, I feel horrible. I am never drinking again, ever.'

'Why did you start?' Safa asked.

Orla pushed herself up on her elbows. 'Because I was

humiliated and embarrassed and I wanted to forget about everything.'

'I guess that didn't work out too well,' Ruby said. She didn't want her sister to drink again. It was bad for you and she didn't want her mum and dad to worry about Orla getting into trouble.

Orla glared at her. 'I've had the worst night of my life. I know I was a total idiot to drink. Can you please not give me a hard time?'

Ruby muttered, 'Sorry.'

Safa patted Orla's arm. 'You'll feel better tomorrow after a good night of sleep. This seems like the biggest thing ever, but really it isn't. This boy doesn't deserve you; he's obviously weak and easily influenced. You deserve better.'

Orla blew her nose. 'Thanks, Safa. How did you get to be so grown up? I feel like I'm talking to an adult right now.'

Safa smiled. 'Life experience.'

Orla reached over and hugged her. 'You must have had a rubbish life. I hope it gets better.'

Ruby gasped. 'Jeez, Orla, don't say that. Her life isn't rubbish.'

Safa laughed. 'It's OK, Ruby. My life was good until three years ago. Even though there was a war in Syria, our town was not affected. But then everything changed and bombs began to fall out of the sky. Since then there have been many bad parts. But Baba always says, "Bad times can't last for ever."'

Orla sighed. 'I used to think that, but now I'm not so sure.' Suddenly she jumped up from her bed and vomited again into the bin. 'God, I feel like I'm dying.'

Safa smiled. 'Baba also says that alcohol is never the answer to your problems; it only makes them worse,' Safa said.

'He's right,' Orla said. 'I've never felt so sick in my life. Your dad is, like, the smartest man in the whole wide world. He's, like, a total genius, like Alfred Instagram or whatever his name is.'

Ruby rolled her eyes. 'Seriously, Orla, even I know it's Albert Einstein.' Sometimes she wondered if Orla was just really dumb or if she played it up a bit.

Orla sat on the bed and wrapped her duvet around herself. 'Leave me alone. I'm sick.'

'It's your own stupid fault,' Ruby snapped. 'You should never have drunk.'

'Stop talking. You're giving me a headache.'

'I'll shout unless you swear never to drink again.' Ruby was really furious with her sister. If their mum and dad found out, there would be world war three. There was enough drama in the house without this. Besides, she hated seeing her sister vomiting and crying. This wasn't Orla. Orla was tough and together and strong. Ruby needed her sister to stay strong. With Mum already falling apart, she couldn't stand it if Orla broke too.

'I swear, I swear.' Orla held up her hands. 'Just be quiet, pleeeeease.'

Safa stood up and told Orla she hoped she felt better soon. 'I have to go – Mama will be worried about me.' She left the sisters sitting on opposite beds, glaring at each other.

Orla peeled off her damp clothes and put on her pyjamas. She then snuck out to the bathroom with the vomit bin and rinsed it out. Ruby sprayed deodorant around the room so her mum wouldn't notice the smell of puke.

Orla came back and curled up in bed. She switched off the light and said quietly, 'If you breathe one word of this to Mum or Dad, you're dead.'

Ruby rolled her eyes. As if!

'And don't worry, I swear on my life that I will never, ever, ever drink again as long as I live.'

Ruby smiled in the dark. Her sister had learned her lesson.

Ruby, Denise and Clara were in Clara's house, eating brownies that Mimi had made. Mimi was, as usual, watching TV shows in the lounge.

Ruby thought Clara's mum should know that she was paying Mimi to do basically nothing. She cleaned the house, which wasn't hard because Clara's mum was, like, super neat and tidy, and then basically she watched TV all day.

But Clara said she pretended that Mimi was a brilliant minder because she liked being left alone. 'Having my mum on my back all the time about schoolwork is enough. I like the fact that Mimi basically ignores me and leaves me in peace.'

Ruby thought it was a bit sad. At least when her mum and dad weren't asleep or with Robbie, they chatted to her. It must be lonely for Clara in the house all the time on her own. Even though Orla could be a right pain, at least she was someone to talk to.

Clara's phone rang. It was a Dublin number. They all froze.

'OMG, this could be the minister. This is it! They found Safa's dad!' Denise squealed.

'Answer it,' Ruby hissed.

Hello?' Clara tried to make her voice deep, trying to sound older. 'Yes, this is she speaking.'

Denise covered her mouth to stop giggling.

'Put it on loudspeaker,' Ruby mouthed.

Clara put the phone down and pressed Speaker. 'My name is David O'Neill,' said a man's voice. 'I work in the Minister's office. We received your letter. We would need further information to be able to look into this matter. For example, what is your friend Safa's father's name? Where in Greece is he? What date did he land in Greece? Do you have his date of birth? Where are Safa and her mother currently living? What date did they arrive in Ireland? What are their dates of birth? We would need copies of their refugee papers ...'

He went on and on and on about papers and documents and dates. Ruby grabbed a pen and tried to write down the things he was saying on the back of a paper napkin. There was such a long list of things they needed to find out. Her head was melted. How on earth were they going to get all this information?

Clara kept her cool. 'Yes, well, that's no problem at all. I will revert with all of those documents ASAP,' Clara said, imitating her mother. She hung up.

They all squealed.

'What are we going to do?' Clara gasped.

'We're never going to find him,' Denise said. 'Forget it. It's too complicated.'

'No way!' Ruby said, louder than she'd intended. 'We are not giving up. Safa needs her dad.'

'Not everyone needs a dad,' Clara said, hands on hips.

Dammit. Ruby hadn't meant it like that. She knew it bothered Clara that she had no dad and usually Ruby was way more sensitive. 'I know, Clara, but Safa's had such a bad time that I really want to help her.'

Denise backed her up. 'Me too, and you're right, we're not giving up.'

'OK, but how are we going to get all this information?' Clara asked.

'Maybe we should just tell Safa?' Denise said.

'No.' Ruby was adamant. 'Safa has had too many disappointments; we can't get her hopes up.'

'Maybe he's dead,' Denise blurted out.

Clara and Ruby stared at her.

'What? I'm just saying it's a possibility.'

'He isn't. I just know it,' Ruby said. She was not going to believe for one second that Safa's dad was dead. No way.

Clara chewed on her thumbnail. 'Well, he could be. Lots of refugees die trying to move countries. I saw this documentary on it – people drown on the boats trying to get to Greece or they die in the back of lorries going from France to London or they die –'

'Stop it!' Ruby shouted. 'He's not dead and that's it. We are going to keep looking and looking until we find him.'

'OK, calm down.' Clara bit into a second brownie. 'We'll have to be really clever about getting all the information we need. We'll each have to ask Safa different questions and sound really casual. So just be all, "Oh hey, Safa, I'm really into star signs … what dates are all your family born?", or something like that.'

Ruby thought that was actually a really clever idea.

'OK, I'll do that,' Denise said. 'My mum is actually into all that star sign stuff, so I know a little bit about it.'

'I'll ask about when she got to Ireland and where her dad is in Greece and all those questions. You're going to have the hard part, Ruby, because you're her best friend. You're going to have to get copies of the refugee papers.'

Ruby stared at her. 'What? How am I going to do that?'

'Go to her house and when she's in the kitchen with her mum, go and look in drawers and find them.'

'Yeah, like a detective,' Denise giggled.

'Thanks a lot, guys. I get the really hard part. I can't go around rummaging through her mum's private things.'

Clara crossed her arms. 'Well, you're the one who started this whole thing.'

'She's right,' Denise said, 'and you're the one who wants to find Safa's dad the most.'

They were right, but still, how on earth was she going to find all the documents in Safa's house? You couldn't just stroll into someone's home and start rooting about in their drawers. Ruby would have to be clever about this. Like a real live detective. But how was she going to do it? How was she going to distract Safa and Rima long enough to rummage about in their house? It was going to be really hard.

But Ruby wasn't a quitter. She wanted to do this for Safa, so she'd just have to figure it out ... somehow.

CHAPTER FOURTEEN

Safa

Safa heard the sound of the plane before anyone else. She felt her heart begin to race and her body begin to shake. The palms of her hands were clammy. The sound of planes terrified her. Planes were bad news. Planes were bombs and death and destruction. Planes had killed her auntie and her uncle and her cousins. Planes had destroyed her school. Planes had killed so many people in their neighbourhood. Planes meant danger, serious danger.

The girls looked up in the yard as a low-flying plane flew above them. 'Hope you're going somewhere hot!' someone shouted up at the sky as they all shivered in the November cold.

Safa had to move. She had to get to safety. Her legs felt heavy, but she forced them on. She had to get away from the sound of the plane.

She raced down the school corridor, burst through the classroom door, rolled under a desk in the corner and hugged her knees tightly to her chest. She was rocking back and forth, trying desperately to push away the horrible memories of bombs falling, when she felt a hand on her arm.

'Are you OK?' Ruby asked, crawling in to sit beside her. 'Was it the plane?'

Safa's voice was hoarse. 'For me planes are danger. Planes killed people I love.'

'But not here. Not in Ireland. In Ireland planes are just bringing people on holidays. It's not like Syria, Safa. You're safe here. It's OK.' Ruby put her arm around her friend.

Safa slowly began to stop shaking. 'You're safe, you're safe,' she kept repeating over and over in her head. Her heart began to stop thumping and she felt her body slowly begin to unclench. She rubbed her eyes and tried to push the horrible memories from her mind.

Ruby drew circles on Safa's back with her hand. It was very soothing. 'That feels nice,' Safa said.

'I do this sometimes when Robbie has one of his fits. Most of the time it doesn't work, but sometimes it does.'

Safa gave Ruby a small smile. Ruby's life was complicated too. Living in a safe country didn't mean that life was perfect.

The noise of the plane made Safa think about her father. Was Baba safe? Was he hungry? Thirsty? Lonely? Injured? *Where are you, Baba? I need you*, she thought, wishing it was his big strong arm around her, comforting her.

The two friends sat under the desk in silence until they heard footsteps and saw two pairs of shiny patent shoes in front of them.

'OMG, are you actually afraid of a stupid plane? Like, seriously. What are you, two years old? Pathetic,' Amber sneered.

Ruby shot out from under the desk. 'Shut up, Amber. Safa's had planes drop bombs on her, so of course she's afraid of them.'

'They didn't actually drop on her, though, did they?' Amber said. 'If they'd dropped on her, she'd be dead.'

'A little sympathy would be nice. Safa's had a really hard time,' Ruby hissed.

'I'm allowing her to live in my country, amn't I? I'm allowing her to go to my school, amn't I?' Amber snapped. 'What more do you want? Am I supposed to give her my clothes? She wouldn't wear them anyway. She only wears horrible baggy clothes.'

'That's because of her religion,' Ruby said.

'My dad says we need to stop letting refugees into Ireland,' Chrissie said. 'They're taking all our jobs and they'll take over the country and make us all be Muslim and wear manky clothes and scarves on our heads and not let us eat bacon sandwiches. He said it's dangerous to let too many foreigners into your country.'

'Your dad is an idiot,' Ruby said.

Safa stood up beside her friend. 'It's OK, Ruby. I've heard all of these comments before. You know, Chrissie, all I want is for my family to be together, to get an education and to work hard and live in a safe place. I don't want to take over anyone's country and I don't care what anyone else eats or wears.'

'Yeah, well of course you're going to say that. My dad says refugees are sneaky and they pretend they're your friend while they're actually stealing your money and taking your job.' Chrissie was not backing down.

Safa felt herself growing angry. 'My father always taught me that we should respect everyone, no matter where they come from or what they believe.' How dare this girl be so rude? How dare she accuse refugees of such awful things?

'Yeah, well, my dad said we need to protect ourselves,' Chrissie snapped.

'The only person you need to protect yourself from is your stupid dad!' Ruby shouted.

'What's going on here?' They all spun around. Mrs Roberts was standing at the door of the classroom. 'Is everything all right, Safa?' the headmistress asked.

Safa glared at Chrissie. 'Yes, Mrs Roberts, we were just having a discussion about refugees in Ireland.'

'I hope everyone was being kind and compassionate?' Mrs Roberts asked.

Safa was tempted to tell the headmistress how horrible Chrissie and Amber were being, but she knew it would only lead to more problems. So she bit her tongue. 'It's been very interesting,' she said.

The headmistress nodded. 'Right, well, I'm delighted that you are having such important conversations and that you are all clearly learning a lot from having Safa in the class. Miss Ingle and I feel that having Safa in the school is an excellent opportunity to open the minds of all the girls to the fact that other people have very different and difficult lives. I hope that you are all showing Safa how decent and welcoming Irish people are.'

Safa wanted to laugh. If only the headmistress had arrived a few minutes earlier and heard Chrissie's vicious comments.

Chrissie's face was red. She was looking down at the floor.

The headmistress left the room. Ruby turned to Chrissie. 'You're lucky Safa is a nice person. She could have got you into a lot of trouble. Next time you have something nasty to say, shut your big mouth.'

Safa was so proud of Ruby. She was being so brave, standing up to these rotten bullies. Ruby grabbed Safa's arm and they went back outside. Denise and Clara were chatting in the corner of the yard.

'You're not going to believe what Chrissie said to Safa!' Ruby said.

They filled the other girls in.

'Wow, Ruby, I can't believe you shouted at Amber and Chrissie. Good for you.' Denise was impressed.

'It's about time everyone stood up to them. They're horrible and ignorant,' Clara said. Turning to Safa, she said in a very serious voice, 'I apologise on behalf of the people of Ireland for those rotten cows and their racist comments. We love having you here.'

Safa giggled. Clara looked so serious. 'Thank you. I accept your apology.'

'I apologise for them too,' Denise said.

'Me three.' Ruby grinned.

The girls giggled. Then out of the blue, Denise said, 'Actually, Safa, we were just talking about star signs here.' Denise winked at Ruby, who went a bit red. Denise turned to Safa. 'My mum is obsessed with them, so I always have to find out what everyone's is. I can't believe I never asked you before.'

'Yeah, she's obsessed,' Ruby said.

'Totally obsessed,' Clara added.

Safa thought Denise's mum sounded a bit strange. Denise said she shouted all day long, because the four boys drove her crazy, and now she was completely obsessed with star signs.

'What star sign are you?' Denise asked Safa.

'Cancer.'

'Oh yeah, that's April, right?'

'No, it's July.'

'Oh yes, sorry, I got mixed up. What date?'

'The eleventh.'

'And how about your Mum and Dad?' Denise asked.

'Aries and Pisces.'

'Right, yeah, so what exact dates? My mum says if you know the exact dates you can really tell a lot about a person.'

Safa thought it was odd that Denise wanted to know her parents' star signs, but then a lot of things in Ireland seemed strange.

'Mama is the tenth of April and Baba is the fifteenth of March.'

Denise wrote the dates down on her hand.

'Couldn't you have brought a copybook out with you?' Clara glared at her.

'I forgot.' Denise shrugged.

Clara pulled a copybook out of her bag and wrote the dates down. 'Speaking of your parents,' she said, 'where exactly is your Dad in Greece? Like what part?'

'He's in Athens. Well, that's where he was the last time we heard from him, but … but that was almost two months ago.'

Clara wrote 'Athens' down beside the star signs. 'Was it any particular area in Athens, or, like, a specific refugee camp or anything?'

'It was a place run by the Red Cross in the centre, I think. I don't really know.'

Clara wrote 'Red Cross' and 'centre of Athens' in her notebook.

'Why are you asking?' Safa was suddenly suspicious.

'Oh, it's just that my mum was asking me about you and how you were getting on and all that and I realised that I didn't know much about your parents and stuff and Mum said it's important to be interested in people and … and …' Clara trailed off.

'And not just be all about yourself,' Ruby added.

'Yeah, like, all "Me me me",' Denise said.

'Exactly, so I just thought I'd ask you more about yourself. Like, for instance, what date did you arrive in Ireland?'

Safa didn't like all the attention and the questions. She preferred just to sit back and listen to the girls chatting. The three of them were staring at her and Clara was holding her pen in the air, waiting for an answer. It felt like an interview or even an interrogation.

Safa fidgeted with her watch strap. 'I don't know, it was last winter, January, I think.'

'Do you think it was the first week, or maybe into the second week?' Clara pushed for more information.

Safa shuffled uncomfortably. 'I don't know.'

'Did you come on a plane from Athens to Dublin?' Clara asked.

'Yes.'

'OK, and then what happened?'

Safa stood up. 'I don't really remember, it's a bit of a blur.'

'I understand. I just thought you might be able to remember some things,' Clara urged.

Safa wrapped her arms around her stomach protectively. 'I don't know.'

'Stop.' Ruby stepped in. 'She's answered enough questions.'

Clara glared at Ruby. 'I'm just interested in the details, Ruby. They are very important.'

'I know, Clara, but Safa has said she doesn't remember, so drop it.'

'Fine, but it's on you.' Clara snapped her copybook shut and stomped off, followed by Denise.

Safa turned to Ruby. 'What's going on?'

Ruby shrugged. 'Dunno, just forget it. Clara can be a bit over the top sometimes. Her mum is a bit intense, so I guess Clara just wants to show her that she has talked to you about your life.'

Safa hoped she hadn't annoyed Clara. She liked her. Clara was bossy and she did ask a lot of questions, but she was kind too and had been a good friend to Safa. But she couldn't remember the exact dates, and surely Clara couldn't be angry with her for that?

Ruby

Ruby opened the fridge. There was a ready-made meal with her name on it and another one for Orla. Mum had taken Robbie to the Children's Hospital in Dublin for a check-up and wouldn't be back until late.

Ruby didn't want a microwave dinner. She wanted a proper dinner. She wanted Mum's amazing spaghetti bolognese, or she wanted her yummy roast chicken and mashed potatoes dinner.

But Mum rarely seemed to have time to cook any more. She cooked for Robbie and often had to cook several meals for him, because depending on his mood he could turn two or three plates upside down. So when it came to Ruby and Orla, they usually ended up with plain pasta, toast or a microwave dinner. If Dad wasn't out in his taxi, like he usually was, he sometimes made them dinner. Orla was supposed to cook, Mum said she was old enough and that if you could read you could cook, but she never wanted to.

As Ruby peeled the plastic off her dinner, Orla came in.

'Oh God, not chicken pesto again. I told Mum I hate that one,' she groaned.

Ruby shrugged. 'There's nothing else unless you want to go to the shops and cook something.'

'I've just spent eight hours in boring school and walked home in the rain. No, I do not want to go out again.' Orla threw her bag down and peeled off her wet coat. 'I guess it's toast and peanut butter again.'

She slammed two pieces of bread into the toaster. Ruby knew when her sister was like this, the best thing to do was say nothing.

'I had to listen to Kylie Phelan telling everyone how

she and Conor are now dating. Stupid cow. I hate her and I hate him and I hate my life. I might as well just become a nun. No guy is ever going to go out with me because we are a "retard family".'

Ruby felt the chicken stick in her throat. She picked up her glass of water and drank to dislodge the meat. 'Do you really think that's what people think of us?' she asked.

Orla spread peanut butter over her toast. 'Yes, I do. We might as well be nuns because no one will marry us because they'll be afraid that we will have kids like Robbie.'

'But Robbie was just unlucky,' Ruby said.

'I know that, and you know that, but people out there are so stupid, they don't understand.'

Ruby put her fork down. She didn't feel hungry any more. 'But most people aren't stupid.'

'In my opinion, they are.'

Ruby reckoned that Orla thought that because the people she hung around with were not the smartest. But she didn't want to say that.

None of Ruby's friends thought that she was from a 'retard family'. Orla was just upset because Kylie was being so nasty. And, besides, who cared what an ignorant fool thought? Kylie's opinion didn't matter.

'Anyway,' said Orla, 'there was one small bright light in my otherwise crappy day.'

'What?'

Orla smiled. 'Kylie's phone went missing and then someone found it floating in the loo.'

'Wow, and how did it go missing?' Ruby grinned.

'I dunno, I guess someone must have sneaked it out of her bag when she was banging on about her new boyfriend. Now, it's ruined, and she can't text Conor.' The sisters laughed.

'You're mad, Orla.'

'She'll have a new phone tomorrow, her parents are loaded, but at least I got a little bit of payback.'

After dinner Ruby went over to Safa's to practise for the play. They had less than four weeks before the big performance and she kept forgetting her lines. Usually Safa came to her house, but she'd invited herself over to Safa's because she needed to try to find the refugee papers.

Originally, she was going to take them, copy them and then put them back, but then Clara had come up with a better idea.

'What if they notice that they're gone?' Ruby had asked Denise and Clara.

'They won't,' Clara had said. 'They probably never use them, like we hardly ever use our passports.'

Ruby hadn't used her passport since Robbie was born. Before Robbie they had gone camping in France every year. It had been brilliant. Dad barbecued every night and they made friends with kids from other countries and the pool had a big swirly slide that they could fly down. There were tennis courts and a big area with table tennis tables and air hockey tables and an ice-cream fridge … it was the best fun. Mum and Dad were always smiling and laughing, and they had been a real family. But Robbie didn't react well to change, so they never went away now. Sometimes Ruby would take Dad's phone and look through all the old photos, the 'before Robbie' photos, and feel sad because they all looked so happy, and Mum and Dad looked so much younger. Ruby wondered if she'd ever use her passport again.

'What if her mum catches me taking the papers?' Ruby had asked.

'Just say you were looking for something to write on,' Denise had said.

Ruby had thought that was a really stupid idea.

'I've got it!' Clara had shouted. 'We don't need to take them. Just take photos of the documents on your phone and then we can print off the photos in my mum's office.'

Brilliant. Clara was a genius. Ruby felt a little less stressed after that conversation. But she still had to find the papers and photograph them. It wasn't going to be easy.

Ruby knocked on the door. Rima answered. Ruby knew Safa's mum from the school yard, where she picked her up every day. She was super nice. Her English still wasn't great, but she always smiled and said a big hi to Ruby.

Safa said that her mum sometimes had bad days when she just stayed in bed, but that thankfully they didn't happen too often. Ruby's mum had lots of bad days when she sobbed in the bath and didn't think Ruby could hear her, so she knew how bad days felt.

'Hello, Mrs Karim,' Ruby said.

'Hello, Ruby, welcome. Are you wanting food?' Rima asked her.

'Oh, no thank you, I ate already,' Ruby said, although the smell coming from the kitchen was so good that she wished she could eat.

'Come, come, Safa eating.'

Rima guided her into the kitchen. The hall and stairs and kitchen were so tidy and clean. Ruby looked around. Everything was in its proper place. In her house there was stuff everywhere. Safa's kitchen was warm, and the smell of spices and cooking made Ruby's stomach grumble.

'You want eating?' Rima asked again. 'Come on, much food.'

'Well, if you're sure, OK.' Ruby sat down opposite Safa, who was eating a chicken curry. It looked and smelt delicious. Nothing like the plastic meal that Ruby had half eaten.

'Hi,' Safa said, her mouth full.

Rima put a dish of steaming curry in front of Ruby. 'Eat, eat.'

'Thank you so much,' Ruby said, picking up her fork and taking a large mouthful.

An explosion of flavours filled her mouth. Flavours that she had never known before. It was amazing. A bit hot, but soooooo good.

'Wow,' she said, giving Rima the thumbs-up sign. 'This is delicious.'

Rima smiled broadly and patted Ruby's head. 'Good girl, Ruby.'

'You are so lucky your mum is such a good cook,' Ruby said between mouthfuls.

Safa smiled. 'I know, I love her food. She couldn't cook properly in the camp in Greece and the food they gave us was horrible. It was so nice to taste her food again when we came here. But she finds it difficult to find all the ingredients she needs.'

The two girls continued to eat in silence and Ruby scanned the room. It was a small kitchen with no obvious place to keep important documents. They must be either in the TV room or in Rima's bedroom.

Rima asked Safa something in Arabic. Safa said, 'Thank you for being such a good friend.'

Rima turned to Ruby, and repeated the words, 'Thank you for being such a good friend.'

Ruby felt her face go red. 'That's very nice of you, Mrs Karim. But Safa is a great friend to me too. She's so kind to help me with my lines.'

Rima turned to Safa. She translated for her mother. Rima nodded and smiled. 'Safa is very good girl. You good girl too. You have sick brother. I pray for him.'

'Wow, thank you. That's very nice of you.'

Rima patted Ruby's head and then cleared the girls' plates. Ruby's was wiped clean. She felt all warm and full inside.

As the girls went up to Safa's room to practise, Ruby saw that the door to Rima's bedroom was open. There was a locker beside the bed with three drawers. She bet the papers were in there.

Safa's bedroom was very bare and painted a rotten green colour. Ruby and Orla's bedroom was crammed, stuffed full of Orla's make-up, clothes and shoes, and Ruby's old cuddly toys and books and sparkly pens and markers. Safa's room had a bookshelf filled with books in English and Arabic and a desk that just had a lamp on it. There was a small wardrobe in the corner of the room and then just her bed. It felt like something was missing – stuff. Stuff from her childhood, old cuddly toys, dolls, pictures, cushions … it just seemed very sparse. But one thing did catch Ruby's eye: the photo of a man beside Safa's bed. That must be her dad. Ruby's heart jumped. If she could get a photo of that photo, they could send it to the Department of Justice with all the documents.

They sat side by side on the bed and went over the lines. Ruby had her phone on her lap. After a few minutes she 'accidentally' knocked the script out of Safa's hand. As Safa bent down to pick it up, Ruby quickly snapped a photo of Safa's dad.

Now Ruby just needed to get into Rima's bedroom. She fidgeted on the bed while Safa read out the lines from the play. Ruby kept getting her lines wrong because she couldn't concentrate. She stood up and walked around the room, pretending to try to remember the lines.

Suddenly, she heard the noise of the television in the room below them. Rima must be sitting down and watching TV. Now was a good time to snoop. Ruby needed to get out of the bedroom. She told Safa she needed to use the bathroom. She walked out of Safa's bedroom, closed the door and loudly walked towards the bathroom before turning around and, as quietly as she possibly could, tiptoeing back down the corridor towards Rima's bedroom.

The bedroom, like Safa's, was sparse. Just a bed, a bedside locker and a small wardrobe.

Ruby thought of her mum and dad's bedroom. It was stuffed full of books and clothes and medicine for Robbie and newspapers and bills and medical files. Mum kept all Robbie's medical files, from the day he was born until now, in big black folders on a bookshelf in their room. She said it was vital that she kept on top of things. 'I'm Robbie's voice,' she said. 'He can't speak for himself, so I have to be his voice.' Dad said that Mum knew more about Robbie's condition than any of the doctors. Mum said that Robbie was just another patient to the doctors and specialists, but he was her little angel, and she was there to fight for him and make sure he got the best care possible.

Ruby slowly approached the bedroom. It was dark but she was afraid to turn on the light. She knew she had very little time. She went straight to the bedside locker and slowly opened the top drawer. It squeaked. Dammit. Ruby froze. She listened out for any footsteps. Nothing. She pulled the drawer out and quickly looked through it.

It had books in it and a wallet and a couple of pens and some medicine. She closed it carefully and moved down to the second drawer. This one opened easily without making any noise. It was full of headscarves and a pair of woolly gloves.

There was only one more drawer left. Ruby said a silent prayer: *please let the documents be in this one, otherwise we'll never find Safa's dad.* She held her breath as she opened the bottom drawer.

Bingo! It was full of important-looking papers. Ruby grabbed them and laid them on the bed. She rifled through them. There seemed to be birth certificates, and some of the other papers had 'refugee' and 'permission' and 'authorisation' and 'immigration' and words like that written on them. Ruby had taken her phone out to photograph them when she heard footsteps on the stairs. *Oh my God!* She panicked. Looking around for somewhere to hide, she saw there was only one option. She grabbed the papers and rolled under the bed.

Just as she pulled her right foot in, Rima walked into the bedroom. Ruby held her breath. All she could see were Rima's silk slippers. Rima shuffled about the room and then sat down on the bed. *Oh no.* Ruby watched as Rima's hand bent down towards the locker. Ruby thought she was going to be sick. She covered her mouth.

Rima's hand hovered and then she opened the top drawer and pulled out a book. She sat on the end of the bed and took off her slippers. She began to massage her feet. Ruby was shaking. What was she going to do if Rima lay down on the bed and started reading? What would she do if Rima fell asleep? Would she have to stay here all night?

She knew Safa would come looking for her soon. She'd been gone too long. Oh God, why had she let Denise and Clara talk her into doing this? Why did she have to do the dangerous part? All Clara and Denise had done was ask Safa questions, not risk being found hiding under her mother's bed with her personal papers.

Ruby was sweating now. She thought she was going to faint. How on earth was she going to explain to Rima why she was hiding under her bed holding her private papers?

The bed creaked. Ruby almost cried out, but clamped her mouth shut. Rima stood up and walked out of the room and back down the stairs. Ruby wanted to punch the air and scream with relief. Instead, she opened her mouth and took in big gulps of air. She had to move, fast.

Ruby rolled out, threw the papers onto the bed and, with trembling hands, quickly snapped pictures of all the documents. She didn't have time to go through them to figure out which ones were the most important. Her hands were shaking so much she wasn't even sure if the photos would come out blurry or not, but she didn't care. She snapped photos of all of them and then shoved the papers back into the drawer.

Just as she was coming out of the room, Safa opened her bedroom door. Ruby almost jumped out of her skin.

'Ruby? Where have you been? You've been gone for ages. Are you OK?'

Ruby froze. She was sure her guilt was written all over her face. Safa would know that she had been up to no good. She tried desperately to keep calm. 'Oh right, yeah, sorry. I, uhm, I just saw your mum coming up the stairs, so I was chatting to her.'

'OK, well, come on, we need to run through the whole scene before you have to go home.'

Ruby's legs were shaking as she followed Safa back into her bedroom. She sat down on the bed before she collapsed. She'd never make a good detective or spy; it was way too stressful.

Ruby was so distracted after the whole hiding-under-the-bed drama that she made a complete mess of her lines. She needed to get out of the house. She needed to go home and calm down.

'What's up with you tonight? Are you OK? Is it Robbie?' Safa looked concerned.

Ruby had to come up with an excuse to get out of the house. 'No, Robbie's fine. I just ... uhm, well, actually I just don't feel great.'

'You do look a bit hot. I hope you're not getting that flu that's going around school. You can't be sick for your big night.'

'No, I'm sure it's not that. I just feel a bit sick.' Ruby held onto her stomach. She felt so bad lying to her friend.

'I hope it wasn't Mama's curry,' Safa said.

'Oh gosh no, it was delicious. I'm just really tired and I have a headache. Sorry, Safa, and thanks for all your help. I'll see you tomorrow.'

'Go home and rest. You need your strength. Do you want me to walk home with you?'

'No, not at all. Honestly, I'm fine. It's no big deal.' Ruby grabbed her script and shoved it into her backpack. She swung her bag onto her shoulder and hurried to the door. 'No need to come downstairs with me, I'll just nip out now. Will you thank your mum again for dinner? OK, bye!' Ruby ran down the stairs and out the front door.

The fresh air felt amazing on her hot face. She gulped in big breaths of cold air and headed towards home. It took longer than usual to get home because her legs were still shaking so much. She really hoped the photos would print out OK, because there was no way in hell she was going back to do that again. No way, no how.

Ruby lay on her bed and texted Clara. 'I found them, but it was SOOOO hard. Nearly got caught.'

Clara texted straight back. 'Did you take photos of all the documents?'

Ruby felt annoyed. How about a 'Well done', 'That must have been scary'? Nothing. 'Yes, I did. Hopefully they will be clear enough.'

'What do you mean?'

'My hands were shaking, Clara. It was really stressful!!!!!'

'If they're not clear they're no use.'

Ruby threw her phone across the room in frustration.

'Ouch!' As the phone went flying across the room, Mum came in. It hit her on the foot.

'Sorry,' Ruby said.

Mum came over to the bed and sat down. 'Hi, pet, are you OK?'

'I'm fine, Clara is just being bossy and annoying.'

'She's a good friend, Ruby. Don't waste time arguing. Honestly, good friends are very important. Everyone drives you nuts sometimes, but Clara is a lovely girl and she doesn't have it easy.'

Ruby did not want to get into a big chat about Clara and their friendship. She wrapped her arms around her stomach. 'I'm just grumpy and my stomach hurts a bit. I think the curry I ate at Safa's was a bit spicy,' she lied.

'Ah yes, curries can be hard on the stomach if you're not used to spicy food.' Mum pushed Ruby's hair out of her face. It felt so nice. They so rarely had quiet time together, just the two of them. Ruby smiled up at her. 'How did the hospital visit go?' Ruby asked.

Mum shrugged. 'Fine. No change, nothing new really.' She snuggled down beside Ruby. 'But the good news is that the consultant told me that he'll try to help me get Robbie into Grangepark School, you know the one for children with intellectual disabilities, next year – which would be incredible. God, Ruby, it would change things so much. I'd have time for you and Orla again and I'd be a better mum, and Robbie would be happier, and Dad wouldn't have to work so hard because Robbie would get all the speech therapy and occupational therapy that he needs at school. We could stop paying for all the extra therapy and he'd be stimulated and happy with other kids like him and specially trained teachers … it would be incredible. But I don't want to get my hopes up because there is a very long waiting list. It's the best school in the country and … well, I guess there are a lot of children who need their help.'

Ruby knew that getting Robbie into Grangepark was a huge deal. She'd heard Mum and Dad and Suzie talking about it. Robbie could start in September, when he was five. Suzie said it was almost impossible to get in, but she had helped Mum and Dad fill out the forms. Mum had sprinkled holy water from Lourdes on the envelope before posting it. She said they needed all the help they could get.

She crossed her fingers as she lay beside her mum. *Please, God, let Robbie get in*, she prayed silently.

'Anyway, how is the play going?' Mum asked.

'Good. I mean, it's OK. I keep forgetting my lines but Safa has been amazing at helping me.'

'She's a lovely girl. When you think of all that she has been through it makes you feel a lot less sorry for yourself,' Mum said quietly. 'No one has it easy. Everyone has some mountain to climb in life. No one's life is ever perfect.'

Amber's was, Ruby thought grumpily. She had a rich dad, a mum who was always baking cakes and taking her shopping and buying her cool clothes. She got to use her passport all the time, going on at least three holidays a year, and she had the new iPhone and she had the coolest Pink backpack that her dad had got her in America. And best of all, she didn't have a brother with disabilities and she wasn't a refugee. Amber had no problems. In fact, her life looked pretty perfect to Ruby. If Ruby had Amber's life, she thought, she would be so nice to everyone. She'd never bully people or be horrible to refugees.

Mum squeezed her hand. 'You'll be a fantastic Scarecrow. I can't wait to see you. I promise not to miss it this year.'

'Swear?' Ruby said.

'Swear.'

'Even if Robbie gets pneumonia?'

'He won't.'

'Mum?'

'I swear I'll be there. I'm very proud of you, Ruby. You're a wonderful girl.'

Mum kissed Ruby on the cheek and put her arms around her. Ruby snuggled in closer. It felt so good to have her mum all to herself. She loved being close to her. Ruby knew that if Robbie got sick her mum wouldn't make it to the show, but it was nice to know that she wanted to come. And maybe this year she actually would.

'Mum?' Ruby asked. But her mother was fast asleep. Exhausted from all the mountains she had to climb.

CHAPTER SIXTEEN

Safa

Safa felt the water rising up. She was sinking …
the waves were covering her mouth, her eyes, her
head … sinking … drowning … *Baba, help me
… Baba, where are you?*

Safa jolted awake. She sat up in bed. She was soaked
in sweat. Another nightmare. 'Oh Baba, where are
you?' she whispered.

She opened her curtains and looked out at the
moon. On the night before they left Greece, Baba had

held her tight and said, 'When you feel sad, look at the moon and know that I'm looking at the same moon and thinking of you. We may not be together, but we are connected.'

'I miss you, Baba. I love you and I hope you come and join us soon,' she whispered to the moon.

Safa had helped her mum write letters to the Irish Refugee Council, the Red Cross, government departments and anyone else they could think of, but they all said the same thing – 'It takes time,' 'You have to be patient.'

Safa was sick of being patient. She had been patient when she was squeezed in the back of a smuggler's truck for days travelling across Turkey. She had been patient when she was stuffed onto an overcrowded boat in the middle of the night, thinking they were all going to drown. She had been patient in the camp in Greece when they queued for hours for every meal. She was sick of being patient. She just wanted her family to be back together; was that too much to ask?

She thought about Amber and Chrissie's sneering faces. Treating her like dirt because she was a refugee. They had no idea how difficult life could be. Safa wished her country could go back to the way it was before the war, before the bombs, before the hate and the violence and the fear.

She longed to feel the warmth of the sun on her skin and wake up to blue skies and the sound of Fairuz songs that her parents loved. She yearned to sit beside Baba as he drank coffee and read her interesting news stories from the newspaper. She longed to go to the market with Mama and smell the fresh fruit and spices of home.

Home ... Syria was not her home any more. Safa had to accept that. Before, she had believed they would return, but now she knew that they probably wouldn't. She had to try to make the most of this, her new home. Ireland wasn't so bad. The people, except for a few idiots, were really nice and friendly and kind. It was safe here. The weather was awful and the food had no taste, but in Ireland she didn't have to live in fear of bombs or death. In Ireland she didn't hear bad news every day. In Ireland her loved ones didn't die. In Ireland she could stop being afraid all the time.

One thing Safa had learned over the last few years was that everyone had problems – some big, some small. She had met people from all over the world in the camp in Greece and everyone had a sad story. And even here, in safe, peaceful Ireland, people had problems. Look at

Ruby – her life wasn't easy. So maybe it didn't matter where you came from; maybe some people just had harder lives than others.

Safa snuggled down under her duvet and rubbed her feet together to warm them up. She prayed that Baba would contact them soon and she prayed that Robbie would get into the school that Ruby said would make her family's life better.

If bad things happened to good people, then good things should happen to them too. Safa fell asleep thinking of Baba's smiling eyes and warm hugs.

The next day, St Mary's were playing in a football cup match against their biggest rivals, Holy Cross National.

Denise and Safa had been picked to play. Safa was thrilled to be on the team. When Mr Kowalski, their coach, had told her, she had almost cried. She loved being part of the team. The other girls on the team were really nice and had welcomed her from the first day. All they cared about was football, not where she came from or her background. As far as they were concerned, if you could play football, you were one of them.

As they warmed up, Mr Kowalski gave them some tips. 'Right, Safa, their striker is a big tall girl. She's got a serious boot on her. If it ends up being a one on one, come out of the goal and run at her. Be brave. Don't hold back. Denise, I'm counting on you to score. If you think you have a shot, go for it.'

When they ran out onto the pitch Safa felt very nervous. She was glad they had allowed her to wear her hijab. She had explained to the coach that she couldn't play in front of a crowd of men – dads and brothers – without her scarf on. Mr Kowalski said he didn't care if she came out in a deep-sea diving suit and flippers as long as she saved goals.

Safa ran into the goal and tried to keep warm by stretching and running on the spot.

'What's the story with the goalie?' one of the dads who was standing quite near Safa asked the dad beside him.

'Apparently she's that refugee kid the headmistress insisted on taking in.'

'What? Are those refugee kids taking our girls' places on the sports teams now too?'

'I didn't think Muslim girls were allowed to play sport,' a mother said.

'Yes they are!' Safa wanted to shout. But she stayed quiet.

'They probably only chose her to be kind. You know, to help her fit in,' a dad said.

'Yeah, she's probably rubbish.'

Just you watch, Safa thought, *I'll show you.*

Safa's need to prove herself to the parents watching from the sideline drove her to play out of her skin. She was on fire. She saved six goals, and she charged out when the tall striker was coming towards her in a one on one and tackled her, getting the ball safely away.

Down the other end, Denise scored two cracking goals. The end result was 2–0 to St Mary's.

'Wow, our new goalie is class!' the dad nearest Safa said.

'And plucky,' the other dad said.

'We're lucky to have her,' the mum added.

'She's streets ahead of our old goalie,' another dad muttered.

Safa felt herself fill with pride. She'd shown them. She'd shown them all that she wasn't some refugee taking their daughters' places. She was a good goalie and she deserved to be on the team.

'You're the player of the match!' Mr Kowalski shouted across at her. 'Brilliant performance, Safa.'

Denise ran over and hugged her. Ruby and Clara came running onto the pitch too.

'You were amazing!' Clara said. 'I find football really boring, but I actually enjoyed watching that match.'

'You rocked!' Ruby hugged her tight.

'Safa, Habibti.' Mama came over and hugged her.

'Is this your mum?' Mr Kowalski asked.

Safa nodded.

'You must be very proud of your daughter. She is a very talented goalie.'

Mama nodded. 'Yes yes, proud. Safa good football. She very brave.'

They all laughed. 'Yes, she is, very brave,' said Mr Kowalski.

Safa felt so good. Like she belonged. Like she fitted in. Maybe she'd never fit into the class or the school, but on the football team, she did.

Denise's brothers came over. 'Only two goals? You're rubbish.' They lifted Denise up in the air. 'We want a hat-trick next time, sis!' The oldest and biggest brother turned Denise upside down and began to shake her. The other three began to wrestle each other.

'Put your sister down! Stop behaving like savages!' Denise's mother roared. The she turned to Safa. 'Well done, Safa, you're a brilliant goalie. You saved some unbelievable shots today. Hello, Mrs ... Mrs ... gosh, Safa, I don't know your second name.'

'It's Karim,' Safa said, smiling.

'Mrs Karim, it's very nice to meet you. I'm Denise's mum and mother to these four lunatics too. Safa is fantastic.'

Rima smiled at her. Safa translated. Mama laughed and replied in Arabic.

Safa grinned. 'Mama says that one child is hard work – how do you manage with five?'

Denise's mum laughed. 'I shout a lot.'

Denise and Safa walked back to the dressing room arm in arm. It had been a good day, a great day. If only Baba had been there to see her shine.

CHAPTER SEVENTEEN

Ruby

Clara's mum, Annabelle, ushered Ruby, Clara and Denise into her office building.

'Right, girls, you can get on with your project in my secretary's office. Don't mess about with the files on her desk or move anything. She's cleared some space for you, and you can grab some extra chairs from the board room. I'll be on a conference call for the next hour or so, so keep the noise down, OK? When I'm finished I'll take you all for hot chocolate.'

'Cool,' Denise said.

'Thank you,' Ruby added.

'OK, Mum.' Clara pushed Ruby and Denise into the secretary's office and shut the door. 'Right, Ruby, have you got your phone?'

Ruby pulled it out of her jacket pocket. Clara went over to the desk, took her laptop out of her backpack and plugged it in. 'You need to email me all the photos of the documents and then we'll print them out and see if they look OK.'

'They look blurry on the phone,' Denise noted.

'Yeah, well, her mum was coming, and I didn't have much time, did I?' Ruby snapped. She was annoyed that the girls hadn't been more impressed with her story of diving under the bed and hiding. All they commented on was the fact that the photos looked blurry. They had given her some praise for getting the photo of Mr Karim, though, which was something.

Ruby sent the photos to Clara's email address.

'You guys are so lucky to have phones,' said Denise. 'I wish I could get one. Mum says I have to wait until I'm thirteen.'

'I only have one because my mum is always at work,' Clara muttered.

'I have one in case there's a problem with Robbie, which happens a lot,' Ruby said.

Denise was the lucky one, Ruby thought. She didn't need a phone. Her mum was always at home. She didn't get calls to say, 'I've had to go to hospital with Robbie, and I don't know when I'll be back,' or 'Can you skip athletics after school and come straight home? I need help with Robbie,' or 'Can you go to the shops and pick up food for dinner?' Ruby wished she didn't have a phone.

Denise looked embarrassed. 'Yeah, OK, I guess that's not so great.'

Clara looked up from her laptop. 'Got them.'

The three girls peered at the screen as Ruby's photos appeared. The documents were a little blurry, but you could make out the words and the writing much more clearly on the laptop than the phone. They'd be OK. Ruby felt tension and worry leave her body. Thank goodness she wouldn't have to go back.

'I'll print them out. Now we have to write a letter to put in with the forms. It needs to sound really professional,' Clara said.

Denise picked up a file from the desk and opened it. 'Look at this, this is formal. We can copy some of the words.'

Clara took out paper with her mother's company name on the top and began to write what Denise read.

'Dear Sir, I refer to my phone conversation with you, dated twelfth of November. As I mentioned in the phone call I am willing to pay you –'

'What?' Ruby peered over Denise's shoulder. 'We're not paying anyone, are we?'

Clara took the file from Denise. 'Let me see. OK, I'm saying, "As mentioned in the phone call, I am enclosing copies of the documents you requested and the date of birth and the location of Mr Karim. I am also including a photo of Mr Karim to help you locate him."'

'Locate is a good word, sounds very grown up,' Denise said.

'Please find Mr Karim as soon as possible. His family is –' Clara paused.

'Devastated,' Ruby said.

'Gutted,' Denise suggested.

'Devastated without him,' Clara wrote.

Ruby wanted the people in the Department of Justice to know that Mr Karim was a good man. 'Also, I think you need to say, "He is a good man and will be a great person to have living in our country. He believes that education is freedom, so he is really smart too."'

Clara wrote that bit down.

Denise took the file back and waved it. 'Say this at the end, it sounds really good: "Your immediate attention to this matter will be appreciated. Sincerely …"'

That did sound good. Ruby's stomach did a little flip. Maybe this would actually work. Maybe, just maybe, they could help find Mr Karim and bring him home to his family.

Clara finished writing the letter and showed it to them. Her writing was like a grown-up's, super neat and swirly. It looked very professional. Clara signed her name, then Ruby did and then Denise.

'They'll just think we're lawyers who work here, and I'm putting my mobile number as the contact at the bottom again,' Clara said.

Denise pulled a big brown envelope from the tray on the secretary's desk and they carefully put the copies of the documents, the photo, the list of important dates and the letter inside.

Clara wrote the address of the Department of Justice on the front. Ruby took out three stamps. Clara said they probably only needed two, but Ruby was afraid that a big envelope might need three, so she'd bought three. They slipped the envelope into Ruby's backpack. She was going to post it on her way home.

Clara held out her little finger. They all linked little fingers. 'Pinky promise not to say a word about this to anyone.'

They pinky promised just as Clara's mum walked in.

'Finished the project?' Annabelle asked.

'Yes,' they said grinning at each other.

'Right, girls, I have half an hour before my next call, so let's pop down to Café Graffe around the corner.'

'I thought you only had one call,' Clara grumbled.

'I know, love, but unfortunately they want to talk through some more details.'

'But Mum –'

'Clara, I'm sorry, but when you run your own company you have to work harder than anyone else.'

'But why don't you get someone else to run it and you can just be a normal lawyer?'

'Because I'm proud of what I have built up. When your dad died, all of the responsibility fell to me. I went back to work and built all this up. I want you to be proud of me. You know, girls' – Annabelle turned to Ruby and Denise – 'it's very important in life to be able to work. You never know what's going to happen and you have to be able to go out and get a job to support yourself and your children. The world has changed a lot even since I finished university. Did you know that there are now more women than men with college degrees in Ireland? Isn't that amazing?'

Ruby and Denise nodded while Clara rolled her eyes. She'd obviously heard this speech before. But Ruby thought Clara's mum was right. It was important for mums to be able to work and earn money.

As they walked down the road to the café, Annabelle asked Ruby how Robbie was getting on.

'Oh, he's OK, the same I guess.'

'I hope you're helping your mum out. I saw her the other day wheeling Robbie in town and she looked exhausted. It's important that you and your sister help her out.'

'Yes, I know, we do.'

'God, Mum, give Ruby a break, she's a brilliant sister to Robbie and always helps her mum out,' Clara snapped.

'No need to snap, Clara. I'm just saying that mums do a lot and get very little thanks. Now, tell me all about your project.'

Ruby froze.

'It's, uhm …' Denise fumbled.

'We were told not to discuss it at home and that no parents were allowed to help at all,' Clara lied.

Wow, Clara was a really good liar. Even Ruby kind of believed her.

❖

When Ruby got home, she heard her mum and dad talking in the kitchen. She peered into the TV room. Robbie was asleep on the couch, his mouth wide open.

Ruby was just going to open the kitchen door when she heard her Mum say, 'We'll stop Suzie's speech therapy. It means you can work a few hours less. I'm worried about you, Frank. You look worn out.'

'Sure we're all tired, Fiona. I'm fine.'

'No, you're not. You're going to fall asleep at the

wheel and crash the taxi if you don't get more sleep. It'll be fine, Suzie can show me the exercises she does with Robbie and I'll try to help him with his speech, and then he'll get into Grangepark next year and then everything will be OK.'

'He mightn't get in,' Dad said.

'He will.'

'When do they tell us if he's got in or not?'

'They didn't say, but hopefully early December. It'll be the best Christmas present. He'll soon be in school, getting the help he needs, and I'll have nine to five free to work parttime and cook proper meals and get my life and this family back to normal.'

'Fiona, we can't pin all our hopes on this. If he doesn't get in, we need a plan B.'

'There is no plan B, Frank. If he doesn't get in, I'll have a nervous breakdown. We can't go on living like this. You can't drive a taxi eighteen hours a day. I can't look after Robbie twenty-four-seven and be a mother to the girls. They are being neglected. I never seem to have time for them. I feel terrible. I'm doing nothing right. He has to get into that school. He just has to.' Mum's voice cracked.

'Ok, love, calm down. I'm sure he will. But just in case he doesn't, we need to look at hiring someone to help you out.'

'We don't have any money, Frank. We're barely surviving as it is.'

'I could ask my mother for a loan?'

'No, we already borrowed money from her. It's not fair. She hasn't much. Look, Robbie's going to get into Grangepark and that's it. We're due a bit of luck; surely to God we'll get this break.'

'Yes, sure.'

Ruby's dad didn't sound very sure. She crossed her fingers. *Please please please let Robbie get into Grangepark. Please don't let Mum have a nervous breakdown. Please don't let Dad fall asleep when he's driving. Please let Robbie get into the school so we can get our family back.*

CHAPTER EIGHTEEN

Safa

Safa watched from the back of the class. Ruby hadn't forgotten any of her lines. She was brilliant. It was as if she *was* the Scarecrow. But Amber kept adding 'Oh my God's and 'Like, totally's to her lines. Mr Parson was beginning to get annoyed.

'Stick to the script please, Amber, no extra words.'

'Dorothy's such a boring dork and do I seriously have to wear this costume? I much prefer the one I brought in.' The one Amber had brought in was so short you could almost see her underwear. Mr Parson had told her to take it off and that under no circumstances was she going to wear 'that outfit' in the play. 'I look like an old granny in this stupid dress.'

'You'd look amazing in anything,' Chrissie gushed.

Denise made a vomit face at Safa and they laughed.

Amber flicked her long hair. 'Yeah, well obvs I know that, but still, I'd like to wear something that's not completely disgusting.'

'That's enough, Amber. Chrissie, say your line.' Mr Parson urged them along.

'I shall take the heart, for brains do not make you happy and being happy is, like, brilliant.'

Mr Parson sighed. 'Stop, Chrissie. When Frank Baum wrote this beautiful character, he did not write "like, brilliant". He said, "and happiness is the best thing in the world".'

Chrissie rolled her eyes. 'It's, like, the same thing.'

'No, it is not. Say the lines as they were written, please.' Mr Parson ran his hands through his hair, which was already sticking up all over the place.

Amber cut across them. 'Mr Parson, my mum said she wants six seats reserved in the front row.' She twirled a lock of her blonde hair around her painted fingernail.

'We do not reserve seats. Seating will be on a first-come-first-served basis, as always.'

'Yeah, well, Mum said that because I am the star of the show, she wants front seats.'

'Well, then, tell your mother to come very early to get her seats.' Mr Parson turned and walked over to Ruby.

'It's very scratchy.' Ruby wriggled around as the straw in her costume rubbed against her arms.

'I know, but it looks very lifelike,' Mr Parson said. 'And well done for knowing all your lines. You were word perfect.'

Ruby smiled over at Safa. 'I had a very good helper.'

Denise waved her arms. 'Do I really have to be a Munchkin? Walking on your knees with shoes sticking out is really hard.'

Ruby giggled. Denise looked ridiculous with big men's shoes sticking out from her knees.

Mr Parson took off his glasses and wiped them. 'No complaining about silly little things. Let's focus on getting our lines right.'

Denise hobbled off, grumbling. Then it was time for Amber to sing her big solo.

Although Safa hated to admit it, when Amber sang 'Somewhere Over the Rainbow' it made the hairs on her arms stand up. She had a gorgeous voice.

Later that day they were sitting around after lunch trying to keep warm, huddling up against the radiator in the corridor.

'Only four and a half weeks to Christmas. What are you asking for?' Clara asked Denise.

'Football boots and a small surprise.'

'I'm asking for an iPad,' Clara said. 'What about you, Ruby?'

'A surprise,' Ruby said.

'What about you?' Denise asked Safa.

'Muslims don't celebrate Christmas.'

'What?' Denise was shocked. 'Like, not at all?'

'No, we actually have two big celebrations, Eid al-Adha and Eid al-Fitr, which is at the end of Ramadan.'

'What's Ramadan?' Ruby asked.

'It's a little bit like your Lent. We fast from dawn to sunset.'

'Hold on a minute – fast as in eat nothing?' Denise looked shocked.

'Yes, and drink nothing too.'

'What? But for how long?' Ruby said.

'A month.'

'What?' They all stared at her.

'A month? Are you not starving?' Ruby asked.

Safa laughed. 'We eat in the early morning and in the evening.'

'But a whole month? What if you're playing football and you need a drink of water? I mean, can you not have it?' Denise asked.

'You just drink lots of water at dawn and again at sunset.'

'But ... but that's mad,' Denise said.

Safa shrugged. 'You give up things for Lent.'

'Yeah, but I gave up crisps and Clara gave up jellies. It's not remotely the same.' Denise said.

'You get used to it and at the end of Ramadan we have our "Christmas". We give each other presents and all the family gets together and celebrates. It's so much fun.'

'I can't imagine not eating for a day,' Denise said. 'I'm always hungry. It must be so hard.'

'It actually isn't.'

'I think you're amazing, Safa,' Ruby said. 'You've been through so much and you can fast as well, and you never moan. I tried to give up biscuits last Lent, but then one day after Robbie had had a two-hour meltdown, Mum offered me a chocolate digestive and I took it. Mum lives on coffee, chocolate and biscuits. She says the caffeine and the sugar help keep her going. She could never be a Muslim.'

'Well, I could never become a Muslim either. I need my food,' Denise said.

Safa smiled. 'I guess you never know if you're going to be able to do something until you're put into a situation.'

'My mum says this quote all the time: "A woman is like a tea bag – you can't tell how strong she is until you put her in hot water,"' Clara said.

'Safa's been in lots of hot water so she must be a really strong tea bag,' Denise said.

The girls all laughed.

Safa felt happy. She knew that these girls accepted her

for who she was. They didn't care that she had a different religion, different beliefs and customs. They were her friends no matter what and she knew she could trust them. It felt so nice to have good friends again.

She'd never forget Sarra, Amira and Taqwa, her friends from Syria, but Clara, Denise and especially Ruby were her best Irish friends.

Safa was walking home with Ruby, who was unusually quiet.

'Is everything OK, Ruby?' she asked. 'Is Robbie sick?'

'No, he's fine. I'm just a bit worried.'

'About what?'

'Can I ask you a favour? Will you pray to whoever Muslims pray to that Robbie gets into Grangepark, the school I told you about? We'll find out in about two weeks, and if he does get in, it'll be so amazing. It'll just make everything so much better for him – but also for all of us. Mum will have her days free to work and be a proper mum again and Dad won't have to drive so many hours and … and … well, it just has to happen.'

Safa watched as Ruby fought back tears. 'I really hope it works out for you,' she said.

'It has to.' Ruby looked at her, tears spilling down her cheeks. 'Otherwise I think my mum will break.'

Safa squeezed Ruby's hand. She felt sick in her stomach. If there was one thing Safa knew, it was that nothing in life was ever sure. 'Try to concentrate on the play. It'll help distract you. The counsellor at the camp in Greece told me that distraction is good; it takes your mind away from the bad things and focuses it on more positive things.'

Ruby gave her friend a little smile. 'I will and thanks. Sorry to bore you with my stupid problems when you've got so many of your own. Honestly, Safa, you're so brave and strong.'

Safa smiled. If only Ruby knew. She wasn't brave or strong at all. She woke up most nights crying from terrible nightmares about Baba. 'I think we're all just getting on with what we have to get on with. Everyone has problems.'

Ruby bit her nail. 'I know, but some have more than others. The only problem Amber has is that she can't wear a miniskirt on stage.'

Safa grinned. 'Amber has many more problems; she is not a nice person. Baba always says there is a reason when someone is not nice.'

'Yeah, it's called getting everything you want and being spoilt rotten,' Ruby said.

They giggled.

'Mama's coming to see the play, even though I'm only introducing it. I've explained the story to her, so she understands what's going on,' said Safa.

'Mum and Dad are coming. Orla is looking after Robbie. Well … they said they'll come, but who knows?'

Safa put her arm on her friend's shoulder. 'I'm sure they will.'

Whatever happened, Safa thought, Ruby's parents had to see the play. Their daughter needed them to show up for her this time.

CHAPTER NINETEEN

Ruby

Orla was painting her toenails bright blue when Ruby came in from rehearsing. 'So, how's the play going?' she asked.

'Good, except Amber is a total diva.'

'Yeah, her sister's a nightmare too.' Orla dipped the brush into the blue nail varnish.

'Orla?'

'Yeah?'

'Do you think Robbie will get a place at Grangepark?'

Orla stopped painting her big toe and looked up at her sister. 'Knowing our family's luck, probably not.'

'Really?' Ruby felt sick. Weren't they due some good luck?

Orla shrugged. 'I dunno, Ruby. I hope so, obviously, but I don't think we should all get our hopes up. It's really hard to get into that school and I just think it's better if we expect the worst.'

But for once Ruby wanted to believe that it would happen, that things would change for the better.

'Anyway, are you nervous about your big night?'

'Yes, very. But Safa's been amazing. She's helped me so much.'

'How come she hasn't got a part?' Orla asked.

'She said she didn't want one. She said she was happy to introduce the play and help out backstage. I think she's still a bit shy about being new and a refugee and stuff.'

Orla frowned. 'Why? She's great and everyone seems to like her.'

'Not everyone. Amber and Chrissie are pretty awful to her.'

'Yeah, but they're total idiots who are horrible to everyone, so they don't count.'

Ruby supposed Orla was right. But she did think they were especially mean to Safa.

'Tell her to ignore them,' said Orla. 'They are just pathetic little spoilt bullies who will never get anywhere in life.'

That was easier said than done. It wasn't easy to ignore people who called you names and made fun of you and sneered at you. But Orla was right; they all needed to learn to ignore Amber and Chrissie. 'Is Kylie still going out with Conor?'

Orla grinned. 'No, apparently he got bored with her and dumped her.'

Ruby smiled. 'So he does have a brain.'

'That's debatable, but now he's texting me. He asked if we could meet up again this week.'

'What did you say?'

Orla paused for dramatic effect. 'I told him to go and shove his meeting up his ass, that I wouldn't spit on him if he was on fire and that anyone who believed that "retard genes" were actually a real thing clearly had a brain the size of a pea.'

Ruby giggled. Orla was crazy, but in the best possible way.

'Now, do my left foot, please.' Orla wriggled her foot in front of Ruby's face.

'No way, I'm not touching your disgusting feet.'

'I'll help you do your make-up for the play next week.'

Ruby did want Orla to help her look like a real scarecrow and she knew her sister would do a good job, so she agreed.

She tried to hold her breath as she painted her sister's toes.

They were sitting in Clara's house, in her bedroom. Ruby was lying on Clara's big double bed. The room was huge and really nice. The bed had fairy lights wrapped all around the top end. Clara had a big desk, with a proper desk chair like they had in offices, and a long bookshelf crammed with books.

Denise was trying to do keepy-uppies with a tennis ball, while Clara was organising her sparkly pens in order of colour. Ruby picked up Clara's phone. 'Are you sure you haven't missed any calls?'

'Yes,' Clara snapped. 'I check it all the time. They haven't contacted me.'

'I think we should call him.' Ruby was sick of waiting. It had been three weeks since they'd sent the information. The waiting was killing her. Between waiting to see if Robbie got a place in Grangepark and waiting to find Safa's dad, Ruby was nervous all the time. She had a sick feeling in her stomach pretty much all day long and she was waking up at night sweating and worrying. She felt tired and grumpy.

'How hard can it be?' Denise said. 'We gave them all the details. Surely they just look up a computer or Google Maps or whatever and find him.'

Clara sighed. 'Seriously, Denise, you need to watch the news. There are millions and millions of refugees. Loads of them have no passports or papers. It's really hard to find anyone.'

'They have to find him,' Ruby said. 'They just have to.'

The door of the bedroom opened. It was Clara's mum.

'Mum?' Clara was shocked. 'It's four o'clock. How come you're home?'

Annabelle pointed her finger at each girl and said, 'I'm home because my office just received a call from the Department of Justice asking to speak to Clara, Denise and Ruby about the case of Mr Karim. Would you girls like to tell me what the hell is going on?'

Denise let the tennis ball roll to the corner of the room. Clara closed her eyes.

Ruby stood up. 'It's all my fault. I made the others help me. Don't be cross with them. I just really wanted to help Safa find her dad.'

Annabelle crossed her arms. 'Go on, I'm listening.'

Ruby's voice shook as she filled her in on what they were trying to do.

CHAPTER TWENTY

Ruby

Mum opened the door to Ruby and Orla's bedroom. Ruby and Safa looked up. Fiona leaned against the door frame as if she needed it to hold her up. Her eyes were red and small and she was still in her pyjamas, even though it was nearly eleven o'clock in the morning.

'Are you OK, Mum?' Ruby asked.

'I'm sorry to interrupt, girls. I know you're trying to rehearse for your play, Ruby, but Robbie's been up all night with a cold. I haven't slept a wink. Your dad's in the taxi and Orla's working in the coffee shop. Could you please take Robbie out for a walk? I just need to lie down for an hour. The fresh air will do him good. I've wrapped him up, he's ready to go.'

Ruby really didn't want to take Robbie for a walk. The last time she'd done it, he'd kicked off and screamed the whole way around the park and everyone had stared.

But her mum looked so exhausted she couldn't really say no. 'OK, Mum,' she said.

'It'll be good to get out and we can still practise the lines,' Safa said enthusiastically.

'Thanks, girls, you're the best.' Fiona gave them a tired smile and went to her room for some much-needed sleep.

Ruby threw her script on the bed and pulled on her boots. She stomped out the door and down the stairs. Safa followed behind, holding the script.

'There's no point bringing it,' Ruby said, pointing to the script. 'We won't get a minute's peace. Robbie will probably freak out before we get to the end of the road.'

Safa pulled on her puffa coat and fixed her hijab.

Robbie was waiting in the hall in his wheelchair. He was snugly wrapped up in a coat, hat, scarf and blanket and he had a bag of bread on his lap.

'Hi, Robbie.' Safa smiled at him. 'How are you?'

'Hi hi hi,' Robbie said.

'Let's get this over with.' Ruby pushed Robbie's wheelchair out the door.

'Bye bye bye,' Robbie said as they left the house.

They walked in silence down the road and across to the park.

'Do you want to see the ducks, Robbie?' Safa asked.

'Es es es,' Robbie said.

Safa handed him some bread from the bag. 'You can give them some bread, OK?'

Robbie gave her a toothy grin. Ruby's heart softened. He looked very cute in his blue hat. She felt bad for being grumpy. Poor Robbie, he was stuck in his stupid wheelchair all the time. She bent down and kissed him on the cheek. 'I'm sorry for being grumpy, Robbie. You're a good boy. I love you.'

'I dove you,' he said.

Ruby smiled and kissed him again.

'Again,' Robbie said.

Ruby kissed him again and then began pushing the chair along the path towards the little pond. Safa linked her arm and while Robbie threw half the bread in the direction of the ducks and ate the other half, they went over Ruby's lines.

Everything was going well until they headed out of the park and down the main street.

Robbie had been really well behaved, and Ruby was feeling happy and full of love for him. But then they passed a big dog tied to a lamppost outside a shop. The dog turned its head towards Robbie and began to bark. Robbie's arms and legs shot out in front of him, his head swung from side to side and he began to roar.

Ruby pushed the chair as fast as she could away from the dog, but it was too late. Robbie had got a fright and he was off. He roared, 'No no no no no!' at the top of his voice.

'It's OK, Robbie, the dog's gone now,' Ruby said as she pushed him further down the street. But Robbie kept screaming.

Safa tried to sing to him, but even that didn't help. He was too upset. Ruby pushed faster.

'Oh God, no,' she cried. Heading towards them were Amber and Chrissie. They were staring at Robbie with their mouths open.

Amber grabbed Chrissie's arm and they hurried across to the other side of the road. 'Oh my God, quick,' Amber said.

'How embarrassing,' Chrissie said.

'Imagine if that was your brother!' Amber squealed.

Ruby put her head down to hide her red cheeks. She was mortified that they had seen Robbie like this. She felt ashamed of Robbie and ashamed of herself for being ashamed of her brother. Now they'd tell everyone in school that they'd seen Ruby's brother having a fit. Ruby didn't want people talking about Robbie. She hated this. She hated when Robbie freaked out in public. It was so awkward.

'HI, AMBER!' Safa shouted across the road. 'HI, CHRISSIE!'

'What are you doing?' Ruby hissed.

'I'm not letting them ignore you. It's not right,' Safa said.

Amber and Chrissie started walking faster.

'AMBER, CHRISSIE, HI!' Safa roared.

People were looking at them with Robbie freaking out and Safa shouting. Ruby began to sweat. 'Stop, seriously,' she begged.

'No.' Safa's teeth were gritted.

Amber and Chrissie could see people looking at them. They gave a little wave of their hands and walked quickly away.

With Safa shouting her head off, Robbie had got distracted and started to calm down.

A man, about Ruby's dad's age, came over to Safa. 'Oi, stop shouting at those poor girls and go home to your own country. We don't want you refugees here,' he hissed.

'Those girls are bullies,' Safa said calmly.

'Shut up and go home, you dirty foreigner. And take that stupid scarf off.' The man reached over and tried to pull Safa's hijab off.

Ruby felt rage rise up inside her like a fire. She whipped around to face the man and roared at him. 'How dare you speak to my friend like that? She is the best friend I've ever had. How dare you tell her to go back to her country? Her country is in a war – she had to leave or die. She is a brilliant person and we are lucky to have her here. How dare you come over here and try to bully her, you horrible man?'

A small group had gathered to see what was going on.

'Well said, pet.' A woman patted Ruby on the back.

'Good girl, you tell him,' another man agreed.

'Leave these girls alone, you racist,' an older woman shouted.

The man walked away, and people moved off.

Ruby turned to Safa. 'Are you OK?'

Safa had tears in her eyes. 'Yes, you were amazing. Thank you.'

Ruby shook her head. 'No, you were amazing, not letting Amber and Chrissie ignore me.'

'There are bullies everywhere. We have to stand up to them.'

'You're right. I guess I didn't have the courage before I met you,' Ruby said.

Safa fixed her hijab. 'I'm not brave, I'm just sick of people being cruel to each other.'

Ruby linked her friend's arm. 'Can you come on all my walks with Robbie from now on?'

Safa grinned. 'Yes.'

Robbie looked up at them. 'Again!'

The two friends giggled.

Safa

Orla was backstage putting the finishing touches on Ruby's make-up. She'd done a great job. Ruby looked like a real scarecrow.

'OK, I've got to go now so Mum and Dad can get here in time for the show. Good luck, sis.' She gave Ruby a hug.

'Thanks,' Ruby said.

It was nice to see them like this, getting on well. Safa liked Orla when she was like this – not crazy Orla, but nice, calm Orla.

Beside them, Amber was having her make-up done by a professional make-up artist her mother had hired.

As she walked by, Orla 'accidentally' bumped into the make-up artist, who was putting red lipstick on Amber, and the lipstick went all over the side of her face.

Amber shrieked, 'Oh my God!'

'Oops, sorry,' Orla said and winked at Ruby and Safa.

Later, tension was high backstage. Everyone was nervous. Safa was helping people with their lines and costumes and anything else that needed to be done.

She found Ruby peeking out from the side of the stage. 'My mum and dad are here,' Ruby said. Her eyes were shining. 'They're actually here!'

Safa was so happy for her friend. She had been hoping that Robbie would stay well, so that Ruby's parents could come and see her shine. She squeezed Ruby's hand. 'You'll be brilliant.'

Denise came up. 'I just feel ridiculous.' Her face was painted bright orange and she had shoes tied to her knees.

Safa and Ruby burst out laughing. 'You look hilarious.'

'I wish I wasn't a stupid Munchkin. My brothers will make fun of me for the rest of my life.'

Clara came over dressed in her school uniform. As the narrator she didn't have to wear a costume.

'I should have gone for the part of the narrator,' Denise grumbled.

'You look great, Denise, and you'll make people laugh. Everyone always remembers the characters that make them laugh.' Safa tried to cheer her up.

'Yeah, but not the characters that look dorky. My brothers will be laughing at me, not with me. Next year I'm not getting forced into being a dumb character.'

'Two minutes to curtains up! Places, please!' Mr Parson hissed.

Safa gave Ruby a hug. 'Good luck, you'll be fantastic.'

Safa shook as she introduced the play. She couldn't see the audience because the stage lights were so bright, but she could feel all of the eyes in the gym hall on her. Beads of sweat formed on her forehead. Safa took a big breath in.

'Good evening, everyone. Thank you all for coming. We have chosen *The Wizard of Oz* this year because of its important themes. The Scarecrow wishes for a brain, the Tin Man wants a heart and the Cowardly Lion wants to be brave. What they don't realise is that they already have these qualities inside themselves. We are all stronger, braver and smarter than we know. We hope you enjoy our version of this musical.'

Everyone clapped loudly and a few parents even whooped. Safa exited and stood at the side of the stage to watch the show. She smiled as she watched Ruby shine. The quiet, shy Ruby disappeared, and the Scarecrow came alive. Safa peeked out into the audience to see Fiona and Frank gazing up at their daughter, in awe of her talent.

They clapped the loudest and whooped every time Ruby came onstage. Safa saw Ruby beam with joy. She was so happy for her friend.

Frank and Fiona clapped and cheered as the first half of the musical ended. Safa's phone began to vibrate in her pocket. She looked down. It was a message:

'SOS. Help. Please come now. Don't say anything to anyone. Hurry. Orla.'

When Safa arrived, the house was in chaos. Orla answered the door, sobbing. 'Please help. I can't stand it. He's been screaming non-stop for forty-five minutes.'

Safa went into the kitchen, where Robbie had thrown everything he could reach onto the floor. His face was red and sweaty from his tantrum, and he was roaring at the top of his voice, 'No no no no no no!'

'I've tried everything – *Peppa Pig*, food, sweets, singing, whispering, walking him around outside, but we had to come back in because everyone was staring at us. I didn't know what else to do and I didn't want to call Mum because I want Ruby to have this night, this one night where Mum and Dad see her shine. So I called you. Could you sing to him, please, Safa, could you try? I'm begging you.'

Safa nodded. Of course she'd help. She looked at Robbie; his head was swerving from side to side, but she managed to get eye contact. She began to sing. She had to sing loudly to be heard over his roaring. At first it made no difference but on the second round of the song, he began to shout a little less. He moved his head to look at her. Finally, he stopped shouting and began to listen. Soon, he was quiet.

All you could hear was Orla crying quietly in the corner.

When Safa finished, Robbie roared, 'Again, again!'

So Safa sang the song again. On it went, over and over. She sang it eight times until Robbie finally fell asleep, exhausted from his tantrum and soothed by her singing.

Orla threw her arms around Safa. 'Thank you. Thank you so much.'

'You're welcome. I'm happy I could help.' Safa's voice was hoarse from singing.

Orla nodded and began to sob again. She seemed so upset. Was she always like this when Robbie freaked out? 'Sorry.' Orla wiped the tears from her cheeks. 'It's just today has been a really bad day.'

Safa said nothing; she waited for Orla to continue. Safa knew that sometimes it was better to say nothing and let the other person talk.

'I knew the letter from Grangepark was due about now. So when I saw the postman this morning, I ran out to get the mail. I've been doing it every day this week, just in case. Just in case Robbie didn't get a place. I wanted to get it before Mum saw it. And … and I was right, look.'

Orla handed Safa a crumpled letter from her pocket. Safa unfolded it. It was from Grangepark. It said, 'We are very sorry to inform you that your son Robert Fitzpatrick has not received a place at the school. We had a long list of applicants and unfortunately Robert was not one of the lucky ones. He will be placed on a cancellation list, but we very rarely get cancellations …'

Oh no! Safa's heart sank. She felt sick.

'I have to burn the letter. I want Mum to have a few more days of hope,' Orla croaked. 'This is going to break her. I know it will. Mum was so sure Robbie was going to get a place. It was the only thing keeping her going. She won't be able to take this news. It's going to break our family.' Orla covered her face with her hands.

Safa sat down beside her on the floor and patted her back. There was no point in saying, 'It'll be OK,' or 'Don't worry,' because it wasn't going to be OK. It wasn't going to be all right at all.

CHAPTER TWENTY-TWO

Ruby

A few days after the musical, Ruby, Clara and Denise stood in Clara's mum's posh office with the big glass window looking over the town. In front of them were a man and a woman dressed in dark grey suits, looking very serious. They had big briefcases.

'This is Kevin Kilbride and Mary Gorman from the Department of Justice,' said Annabelle.

Clara moved forward and shook the adults' hands, so Denise and Ruby did the same.

'This is my daughter Clara and her friends, Ruby and Denise, who signed the letter they sent to you on my company notepaper,' Annabelle continued.

Ruby knew they were in big trouble and what they had done was wrong. She had to say something, so she stood forward and blurted out, 'I'm sorry for using your company paper, Annabelle. I know it was wrong, but we just wanted to help Safa so badly.' Turning to the two other adults, she pleaded, 'Can you help us find Mr Karim? Please? Safa is such a brilliant person and she misses him so much. If we are in big trouble it was all my idea so I'm the one to blame. I made Clara and Denise help me.'

'You didn't make me help you, I wanted to' – Clara pulled her shoulders back – 'and I'm not sorry.'

'Me neither!' Denise said. 'We all just want to help Safa.'

Kevin held up his hands to silence them. 'This is a very unusual case. We don't usually receive notes from children written on law-firm notepaper. But we have spoken to your mother and she has assured us that your intentions are very good,' Kevin said.

'We were impressed with your letter and all the information that you sent us – it really helped us in our search. We have been looking into Mr Karim's case,' Mary added. 'There was a file opened on him already as we had received a request from his wife and daughter a while back. I'm afraid we have a very big backlog of cases so we hadn't got to dealing with Mr Karim's application yet.'

Kevin cleared his throat and opened his briefcase. 'As you may or may not know, all applications for family reunification received by the minister after the thirty-first of December 2016 will be processed in accordance with Section fifty-six and Section fifty-seven of the 2015 Act.'

'What is he talking about?' whispered Denise.

'Shhhh, we have to listen,' Ruby said.

Clara held up her hand. 'I am very sorry to interrupt you, Mr Kilbride, but we don't really understand about Sections and Acts.'

Mary smiled. 'Look, girls, there is a process that you have to go through. But because of the creative way you went about trying to get our attention and the passion of your letter, we focused more resources on Mr Karim's case and I am very happy to report that with the help of the Irish Red Cross we have located him.'

'Oh my God!' Ruby squealed.

Mary raised her hand. 'Unfortunately, he is in hospital. He has been very ill and can't be moved just yet.'

Ruby's head was spinning. They'd found him? They'd found Safa's dad! 'Are you sure it's him, like, absolutely certain?' she asked.

'Yes.' Mary smiled. 'A few months ago, Mr Karim was attacked, robbed of his money and all his identity documents. He was left with severe concussion.'

'Oh my goodness, is he going to be all right?' Annabelle asked.

Please don't let him die, not now. Not after they'd finally found him. Ruby held her breath.

Mary nodded. 'Thankfully, things are looking much better now. Whoever attacked him stole his identity papers and his mobile phone. He has been in hospital since then, mostly unconscious. Safa and her mother haven't been able to contact him or find him, because no one knew who he was, and he was unconscious for a long time. But two weeks ago, he regained consciousness and began to remember things. He has improved a lot in the last two weeks and the doctors are very happy with his progress. So, unless there is a setback, we are hoping he will be able to travel soon. So, it is good news.'

Clara burst into tears. Ruby had never seen her cry. Clara turned to Annabelle and buried her face in her mother's shoulder. Annabelle hugged her tight. 'It's OK, love, you found him. You crazy kids found Safa's dad.'

Denise bounced up and down, punching the air. 'We did it, we did it!'

Ruby stood with her mouth open, trying really hard to take it in. They had found Safa's dad and he wasn't dead. He was alive and sick but getting better and he'd be in Ireland before Christmas. Ruby knew Safa didn't believe in Christmas, but still, it was the best Christmas present ever.

Denise threw her arms around Ruby, and Clara came over to join them. They hugged each other tight. 'We did it!' they shouted.

'All right, that's enough of that. I think you have some thank-yous to do,' Annabelle gently reminded them.

The girls shook hands with Kevin and Mary. 'Thank you so much. You have no idea how happy Safa's going to be. This is the best news ever,' Ruby said.

Mary had tears in her eyes. 'I'm glad we could help. Reuniting families is a very important part of our job.'

'Yes, well done, girls. Now, we've been in touch with Mrs Karim to explain all of this and for now, Mrs Karim has asked that you do not say anything to Safa. She wants to wait until her husband is safely in Ireland before getting Safa's hopes up,' Kevin added.

The girls nodded. How could they keep this information to themselves?! It was going to be so hard, but oh-so worth it.

Annabelle walked Kevin and Mary out to the reception and waved goodbye. When she came back in she glared at the girls with her arms crossed and her eyebrows all high in her forehead. 'You are in big trouble. You cannot use my company notepaper to send letters to government ministers pretending you work here.'

'Sorry,' they all said.

'But you are also absolutely wonderful, and I am so proud of you.' She threw her arms around the girls and hugged them. 'You should all consider becoming lawyers. I think you'd make very good ones. Now, I am taking the rest of the day off to take you out for pizza and ice-cream.'

Clara stared at her mother. 'What? Are you serious?'

Annabelle put her hands on Clara's cheeks. 'Yes, love, I am. This has made me realise that I need to spend more time with my incredible daughter and her friends. I'm too wrapped up in work; I want to know what's going on in your life. You'll be eighteen in seven years and gone off to college. I want to be there for you more.'

Clara put her arms around her mother and squeezed her tight.

Ruby felt all warm inside. She wanted to run home and hug her own mum. She wondered if she'd be proud of her when she found out. She hoped so.

CHAPTER TWENTY-THREE

Safa

Safa woke up in the middle of the night, for once, not from a nightmare. She woke up and made a decision. She was going to help Ruby and her family. She was not going to let them break.

Later that day, Safa found herself standing outside a big, heavy wooden door. She took a deep breath and pushed it open. She walked into the reception area. There was a woman working on a computer behind a desk.

'Hello,' Safa said in her most polite voice. 'I'd like to speak to Mrs Peabody, please.'

The lady behind the desk asked her if she had an appointment.

'No, I don't.'

'Well, then, I'm afraid you'll have to come back another day. Mrs Peabody is very busy.'

Safa clenched her fists. 'I'm sure she is, but I'm not leaving until I speak to her. It's an emergency.'

The receptionist smiled a thin-lipped smile. 'What kind of emergency?'

'I'd like to discuss that with Mrs Peabody,' Safa said, trying to sound as grown up as she could.

'Mrs Peabody is busy, young lady.'

'I'm sorry, but I must insist on seeing her.'

The receptionist's face turned red. 'As I said, she is not available. I must ask you to leave now.'

'I will not leave until I speak to her. If you try to make me leave, I'll shout and scream the place down.'

The woman stood up from her chair and leaned over. 'How dare you?!'

'I'm sorry but I have to speak to Mrs Peabody, and

I'll do whatever I have to do to make that happen.'

The receptionist came around from behind her desk and grabbed Safa by the arm. 'Get out this minute.'

'MRS PEABODY, I NEED TO SPEAK TO YOU, THIS IS AN EMERGENCY!' Safa roared at the top of her voice. Her throat still hurt from all the singing she'd had to do on the night of the musical to calm Robbie down.

A door opened and a woman popped her head out. 'What on earth is going on?'

'This young hooligan is causing a scene,' the receptionist snapped.

'Are you Mrs Peabody?' Safa asked.

'Yes.'

'I need to speak to you – it's an emergency. Please, just give me five minutes of your time.'

'All right, well, you'd better come in before you make any more fuss.'

Safa followed Mrs Peabody into her office and sat down in a chair opposite her.

'I think you'd better explain what this is all about.' Mrs Peabody sat back and waited for Safa to speak.

Safa squeezed her hands together and took a deep breath. She had to get this right; she had to make this work. 'My name is Safa Karim. I have travelled from Syria with smugglers; I almost died twice. I haven't seen my father in a long time and in the last few months I have had no contact with him at all.' Her voice began to crack but she managed to get her emotions under control. She had to be strong now. 'The one person who has been my guardian angel since I came here, my real true friend, is Ruby Fitzpatrick. Her brother Robbie – Robert Fitzpatrick – needs a place in your school and you sent a letter saying that he wasn't accepted. You need to change that. The family is going to rip apart. Fiona, the mum, is going to break in two if you don't let Robbie come here. They are a lovely family, but they can't take any more. I've seen families pushed to the edge. I've seen families fall apart because they broke. I saw it in Syria; I saw it in the camps in Greece. I am not asking you, Mrs Peabody, I am begging you to save this family. Robbie is a very sweet boy, but he needs help. They can't keep doing it all themselves. Ruby never gets any attention and Orla, her older sister, is really sad but pretends she isn't. You have to help them.'

Mrs Peabody sat back in her chair. 'And how did you survive without breaking?'

'I guess I'm a strong tea bag,' Safa said.

Mrs Peabody frowned. 'I don't understand.'

'My friend Clara says that a woman is like a tea bag – you can't tell how strong she is until you put her in hot water.'

Mrs Peabody laughed. 'That is a very true saying. You are a very brave young girl.'

'Well, I'm lucky too. I have parents who love me, and I have made really great friends here – Clara, Denise and Ruby. But Ruby is my best friend and I have to help her.'

'I'm sorry, Safa, but I can't help you. There is nothing I can do. The school is full for next year. Unfortunately there just aren't enough schools that cater for children with disabilities, so the waiting list is long.'

Safa dug her nails into the palms of her hands. She had to keep trying. She was not taking no for an answer. 'My father always says there is no such thing as "can't", only "won't". You have to help, Mrs Peabody. I'll come and sing to the kids – Robbie loves my singing. I'll help feed them and I'll clean up for free. Please, Mrs Peabody, you have to help Ruby's family. I'll do anything you ask.'

Mrs Peabody looked at Safa for a long time. 'You really mean that, don't you?'

'Yes, I do.'

'I don't think I've ever met a more courageous or compassionate person than you. What you are doing for your friend and her family is really exceptional. They are very lucky to have you as a friend, fighting their corner. I'll tell you what I'll do. I will look at Robert's application and see if I can do something to help the family. I can't offer him a full-time place, but I promise to do everything I can to figure out a way to help the family.'

Safa leant forward. 'Do you promise?'

'Yes, Safa, I promise.'

'Well, then, I know you will fix this. I know you won't let this family break.'

Mrs Peabody smiled. 'You'll go far in life, Safa. With the passion and compassion you have, you will reach the stars. Your family should be very proud of you.'

'Thank you. I won't take up any more of your time.' Safa stood up and politely held out her hand.

Mrs Peabody shook it. 'You are a very special girl. Don't ever change.'

Safa left the school feeling lighter. Maybe, just maybe, she'd been able to help.

CHAPTER TWENTY-FOUR

Ruby

Ruby had been standing at the kitchen window for nearly an hour. Dad had called to say the flight was delayed, but they should be back by two o'clock. She'd been afraid to move in case she missed them arriving. She wanted to be there to greet them.

Ruby could hear her mum upstairs trying to get Robbie down for a nap. They all wanted Robbie to be asleep and not cause a fuss, but by the sounds of things, he was having none of it. Ruby could hear a muffled 'No no no no!' from his bedroom.

Then she saw it. Her dad's red taxi. *Oh my God, they're here.* Ruby's heart leapt as she saw the car pull up outside the house. Her dad jumped out and rushed around to open the passenger door.

Slowly, so very slowly, a man climbed out. Ruby's dad held him up on one side and helped him steady himself. Safa's mum was on the other side, holding his hand. Ruby gasped. Mr Karim, Baba, was here, in Ireland, outside her house. Safa was going to get the best surprise ever. It was all very real now. Ruby stared and stared. He was not like she'd imagined at all. He was very skinny, his hair was white and he had black shadows under his eyes.

'Crikey, he looks wrecked.' Orla came up behind her. 'There's no way he's going to be able to eat all this mad food. I'd say he'll be full after three olives.'

Behind them, on the kitchen table, was a feast of spicy food. Fiona had gone into overdrive, googling Syrian food and cooking non-stop for days.

'I wouldn't mind if it was nice, but it's manky food. The only good part is the chocolate cake,' Orla grumbled.

Ruby ignored her sister. She was holding her breath as Mr Karim made his way slowly up the path.

Ruby rushed to the door. She flung it open and there in front of her was Mr Karim, in the flesh. He looked exhausted, but his eyes – his eyes were Safa's eyes, all bright and shiny, and they twinkled at her.

Dad helped Mr Karim up the step and into the hall. Rima gently helped her husband take his coat off.

Ruby tried really hard not to cry. He was here. He was really here. 'Hello,' was all she could croak.

'Welcome home,' Orla said, sticking her hand out over Ruby's shoulder. 'Well, I suppose it's not really home, I mean, Syria is home, right? So it's kind of more of a welcome back to your family, I guess. You'll probably never actually go home with the war and all.'

Ruby glared at her sister. She was such an idiot. Why was she banging on about the war in Syria?

'OK, girls, give Mr Karim some space. We'll settle him in the lounge.' Dad and Rima moved forward and gently lowered Mr Karim onto the couch. Rima fussed over him, plumping cushions behind his back and making sure he was comfortable.

Mr Karim exhaled deeply and then looked up. 'You must be Ruby.' He smiled at her. His voice was strong even though he looked frail.

Ruby was frozen to the spot. Orla shoved her forward. Ruby wasn't sure if she should hug Safa's dad or shake his hand.

While she was hovering, Mr Karim reached up and took her hand between his two hands. They were warm and comforting. 'Ruby, I want to thank you from the bottom of my heart for what you have done for me and my family.' He spoke English like an English person. He even had a posh accent and all. His eyes held Ruby's. She stared into them; they were so full of warmth and kindness.

'Uhm, sure. I mean, you're welcome.'

'I am so grateful that Safa has a friend like you here in Ireland.'

'Well, Safa has been an amazing friend to me too. She got my brother Robbie into this amazing school and it's going to change all our lives.'

'Well, she got him in part-time, but still, it's great,' Orla said. 'Like, seriously brilliant.'

Robbie had been offered a place in Grangepark, five half-days a week, 9 a.m. to 1 p.m., and then after a year of half-days, he would be offered a full-time place. When Mrs Peabody called Mum to tell her, Ruby had never, ever seen anyone cry so much. Ruby thought her granny had died because Mum was so upset, but they were tears of pure happiness and relief.

Mr Karim nodded. 'Yes, your father told me what Safa did, and I am so proud of her. I cannot wait to see my little girl and hold her in my arms.' His voice shook.

Dad came back into the room and handed Mr Karim a glass of water, which he drank deeply from.

'So, like, what happened?' Orla jumped straight in. 'We heard you were attacked and lost your memory. It's like that old Sandra Bullock movie where the guy she fancies bangs his head and she's in love with him and then he thinks she's his girlfriend and –'

'Orla,' Ruby snapped, 'Mr Karim has no idea what you're talking about.' Ruby wanted to shove her sister out of the room. She was being so annoying. Mr Karim did not want to hear about some stupid movie.

'Jeez, I was only saying,' Orla huffed.

'It's all right.' Mr Karim held up his hand. 'Yes, I was attacked in Greece by a gang. I was asleep in a plastic tent when they tried to rob me. I woke up and tried to fight them off, which was not such a good idea when there were four of them against me. I should have let them take my papers and money. I woke up in hospital with severe concussion not knowing where I was, or who I was.'

'That must have been really scary,' Ruby said.

'It was, but no more frightening than having to leave your country in the dead of night and being separated from your family.' He reached over and held his wife's hand.

'I dunno, there are days when I wish I could be separated from my family,' Orla said.

'Don't you have to go and help Mum with Robbie?' Ruby glared at her sister.

'No.' Orla was not going to miss a minute of the excitement.

Thankfully Dad muttered something about helping out and dragged Orla out of the room.

'Sorry about my sister. She can be very annoying.' Ruby blushed. She wanted Safa's dad to think they were a nice normal family, not a bunch of nutters.

Mr Karim smiled. 'I like Orla. She is spirited.'

If spirited meant mad then Ruby agreed, but she had a feeling it was a compliment.

'What time will Safa be here?' Mr Karim asked.

Ruby looked at the clock on the mantlepiece. 'She'll be here in about twenty minutes. Everyone is so excited. We can't wait for Safa to see you. She misses you so much. She talks about you all the time and tells me all the wise things that you used to tell her.'

Mr Karim smiled. 'The wisest thing I have learned over these last difficult months is that the only thing that really matters is family. In the end, they are everything.' He kissed his wife's hand, and she gazed lovingly at him.

Rima's face was glowing; she looked so happy. It was really romantic. Ruby had never seen her dad kiss her mum's hand. Then again, her mum and dad saw each other every day, while this was a big reunion.

Mr Karim stifled a yawn and then rested his head back on the couch and closed his eyes. 'You will have to excuse me, Ruby. I wasn't able to sleep last night because I was so excited about flying here this morning. I just need to rest for a few minutes. I want Safa to see me standing up and strong.'

Rima murmured to him in Arabic and stroked his forehead. He looked wiped out. Ruby worried he wouldn't be able for all the excitement. Maybe they shouldn't have organised a party. Maybe they should have let Safa meet him somewhere quiet, alone. Her stomach flipped. Oh God, had she messed this whole reunion up?

She went out into the kitchen where Robbie, who was wide awake, was banging a wooden spoon on the table.

'Mum!' Ruby groaned.

Fiona shrugged. 'I'm sorry, love, I tried. I think he can sense the excitement and he wants to be part of it. It's either have him here happy or upstairs roaring his head off.'

Ruby stood in front of her brother, her hands on her hips. 'Robbie, this is a very important day. It's a party for Safa, OK?'

'Es.'

'So, you have to be very good and no shouting. Right?'

Robbie scrunched up his nose. 'Es, bye bye, kank you.'

Ruby had no idea if Robbie understood a word she'd said. She prayed that he'd be good and stay calm. There was no way Mr Karim could cope with one of Robbie's fits. The poor man was still so weak. Ruby crossed her fingers.

She felt her mum's hand on her shoulder. 'Nervous?'

Ruby nodded. 'Very.'

'Don't be, sweetheart. It's going to be wonderful. This is going to be the happiest day of Safa's life.' Mum got choked up and dabbed her eyes with a tissue.

Ruby reckoned that her mum had cried more in the last few days than in the last few years, and that was saying something. Since Fiona had found out that Robbie had a place in Grangepark and that Ruby had led the search for Safa's dad, she hadn't stopped crying. Ruby had also never had so many hugs. Every time her mum or dad had seen her over the last few days, they had thrown their arms around her. It was nice and all, but it was a bit intense.

'Oh God, Mum, please stop crying,' Orla pleaded. 'We're all going to drown if you don't stop. For once everything is actually good. We should be laughing and celebrating.'

Fiona nodded. 'You're right, but these are happy tears. Such happy tears. I feel so lucky to have such a … such a …'

'Yeah yeah, such a brave daughter, I get it. You've only said it a zillion times. I'm still here, you know. I am also your child. Between Robbie and Ruby I might as well be invisible.'

'No one could miss you with that tan.' Dad grinned. 'They can see you in space. Luminous, you are.'

'Ha ha.' Orla pretended to push her father away as he pulled her in for a hug.

Ruby looked at her watch. Fifteen minutes to go. She could feel emotion rising up through her chest. Her head was pounding. So many feelings were spinning around – joy, fear, excitement, nerves, relief, worry, happiness … it was a whole mixture and it was churning around and around. She so badly wanted this to go perfectly.

She took deep breaths and tried to keep calm.

The doorbell rang. They all jumped.

'Helloooooo, it's us! Sorry we're late. Clara insisted on getting changed three times!' Denise shouted through the letterbox.

Ruby opened the door and the three friends hugged and squealed. It felt good to release some of the tension.

Annabelle shooed them inside. 'Quick, Safa will be here soon.' She closed the front door and went into the kitchen.

'Is he here?' Denise whispered.

'Yes, he's in the TV room,' Ruby said.

'What does he look like?' Clara asked.

'Well, he looks kind of old and sick, but happy too.'

'Can we meet him?' Clara asked.

'He's resting. He has very little energy. And he really wants to be able to stand up and walk when Safa arrives.'

Clara was not letting go. 'Can we peep in? I just want to see him.'

Ruby knew Clara would keep pressing, so she and her two friends tiptoed towards the lounge and peeped in. Mr Karim still had his eyes closed.

'He looks like my granddad.' Denise was shocked.

'Yes, well, he's been through hell, remember, so obviously he's not looking his best,' Clara reminded her.

'I know that. I'm just saying,' Denise hissed.

Rima spotted them and came to the door.

'Sorry, Mrs Karim, we just wanted to say hello,' Clara whispered.

'Well, Clara insisted. I was happy to wait,' Denise said.

'Is he going to be OK?' Clara asked. 'Safa will be here any minute now.'

'Mr Karim very tired. But he wake up for Safa.' Rima smiled. 'Love make you strong. Mr Karim strong for Safa. You see.'

She was right, Ruby thought: love did make you strong, and brave and fearless.

CHAPTER TWENTY-FIVE

Ruby and Safa

The girls all stood in the kitchen, holding hands, watching the clock tick.

'My stomach is doing backflips,' Clara said.

Denise was jigging about, unable to stay still.

Ruby was trying not to throw up.

Dad popped his head around the kitchen door. 'I think I see her coming up the road.'

Clara squeezed Denise's hand tightly.

'Ouch!' said Denise.

'Sorry, I'm so nervous I think I might pass out.'

'Me too,' Denise said. 'I couldn't even eat lunch. Imagine, me not eating. But I'm definitely having some of that chocolate cake your mum made.'

How could Denise think about food? Ruby was afraid to open her mouth. She felt so many emotions, she was afraid that if she spoke she'd end up crying. So she clamped her mouth shut and said nothing.

Mum was chatting to Annabelle and feeding Robbie Smarties to keep him quiet.

Orla came over and poked Ruby in the back. 'Are you ready?'

Ruby turned to her sister and nodded.

'Nervous?'

'Very.'

'It'll be fine. Chill. You're a bit of a legend, Ruby.'

Ruby stared at her sister. 'What?'

Orla popped a Smartie into her mouth. 'I know I don't say it much, but what you've done is pretty amazing. I'm proud of you, sis.'

'Thanks!' Ruby was shocked. It was probably the nicest thing Orla had ever said to her.

Orla walked over to the cake, picked a chocolate finger off the side and stuffed it into her mouth.

'Do you think Safa will be happy?' Clara asked.

'I hope so,' Ruby said.

'Of course she will,' Denise said.

The doorbell rang. Everyone froze.

'Well, come on then, someone answer the door! We can't leave her out there all day,' Dad said, nudging Ruby towards the hall.

Ruby's hands were shaking as she opened the door.

Safa stood there beaming. 'Hi.'

'Hi.'

'I bought some chocolates for your mum. I know she likes them.'

'Great, thanks.' Ruby was afraid to say any more in case she blurted anything out.

Clara and Denise came into the hall.

'Act normal,' Clara hissed at Denise.

'Hi, Safa,' Denise said. 'How are you? Are you good? Yeah? All fine? Yeah?'

Safa looked at her strangely. 'I'm fine, thanks. Are you OK?'

'What? Me? Yeah, I'm great. Brilliant. Sound.'

Fiona popped her head out the kitchen door. 'Come on in, Safa love.'

Safa walked in and saw the big feast of food on the kitchen table. 'Oh my goodness!' she exclaimed. 'You've gone to so much trouble.'

'Well, we wanted to thank you for all you've done for this family. You helping to get Robbie into Grangepark is going to change all our lives. You're a very special girl, Safa.' Fiona hugged her.

'Yes, you're a diamond,' Dad added.

'Thank you so much.' Safa's eyes were shining. 'I never expected all of this.'

'You deserve it. You're brilliant.' Orla's voice trembled.

Ruby looked at her sister. There were tears in her eyes. Oh no. Ruby quickly looked away. If Orla cried, Ruby would break down. She couldn't start crying now. Not yet. Not before the big surprise.

Clara nudged Ruby. She cleared her throat. 'Actually, Safa, we have a present for you. It's from me and Clara and Denise,' Ruby said.

'But mostly Ruby – it was her idea,' Denise admitted.

'Yeah, but I did a lot of the work,' Clara said.

'Fair enough, you did, but it was still Ruby who had the plan.'

'I know but still –'

'Girls!' Annabelle cut across them.

'So anyway, your present is here,' Ruby croaked. She looked at her dad, who rushed out of the kitchen.

Safa frowned. What was going on? Everyone was staring at the door. Safa could feel the tension in the room. Her heart began to beat faster. What was the present? What was it? Why was everyone so quiet?

She could hear Ruby's dad saying, 'Easy now, mind your step.'

Then a figure appeared at the door. A man. He was standing in the doorframe, and the light from the hall was behind him. Safa rubbed her eyes. It couldn't be. It just couldn't be. It looked like him, but thinner, older, greyer … but the eyes, the beautiful eyes …

Her legs were shaking so much she thought she'd collapse.

'Hello, Habibti,' he called out to her.

'Baba! Is it really you?' Safa cried out, staggering towards him.

'Yes, it's me.' Mr Karim opened his arms just in time to catch his daughter.

He wrapped her up in a huge hug. She inhaled his scent. Baba's smell.

Was this really happening? Was her father really here, in front of her? Safa pulled back and pinched herself on the arm. 'It is real?'

'Yes, it is,' her father said.

Mama was standing behind him, smiling and crying at the same time. It really was her dad. Baba, he was OK. He was alive, he was here.

'Baba, I missed you so much.' Safa began to cry. All of her fears, worries, and nightmares about never seeing her father again bubbled up from deep inside her and exploded out of her. She cried and cried. Her whole body shook.

Baba held her tighter. Beside her Ruby was sobbing too. Safa looked around. Everyone was crying, even Annabelle, who looked like she never cried. Robbie was shouting, 'Again!' in the corner.

Safa turned to Ruby. 'Thank you. Thank you for the best present I could ever have wished for.'

Ruby gave her a teary grin.

'Kank you, kank you!' Robbie shouted.

Everyone laughed.

It was all right, Safa thought. Everything was going to be all right. Magic did happen. Good things did happen after bad. There was a silver lining in this cloud.

She snuggled closer to Baba and let his arms hold her and keep her safe.

The last day ...

Mrs Roberts stood up in front of the microphone. She cleared her throat and asked for silence.

Everyone stopped chatting and turned to her.

'I have a special announcement this morning. As it's the last assembly before Christmas, this year we have decided to give a special pre-holiday award for courage. It's the first time we've given out this award, but it was suggested to me by one of the girls, and I think it's an excellent idea.'

'Courage.' Amber said. 'I never heard about this award?'

'I bet it's for you,' Chrissie said. 'You're so brave, being the star of *The Wizard of Oz* and always saying exactly what you think.'

Safa, Ruby, Clara and Denise giggled.

'The award is going to a girl who has been in the school for a few years now. She has always been a quiet girl, and little did we all know that underneath that quiet exterior was a heart full of courage. This girl went out of her way to help a fellow classmate. She devised a plan to find this student's missing father.

'This girl contacted the Department of Justice and got them to search for this man. She and her two friends found Mr Karim. They reunited Safa with her father. The recipient of the first ever Medal of Courage is' – she paused for dramatic effect – 'Ruby Fitzpatrick.'

Ruby felt her cheeks burn.

'Go on.' Safa nudged her. 'Go and get your medal.'

'It was you, wasn't it? You told Mrs Roberts to give me this award,' Ruby said.

Safa smiled. 'Yes, I did, because you deserve it, Ruby. You're the best friend I could ever, ever have wished for.'

Ruby's legs felt like jelly as she walked up to the top of the hall and climbed the steps to the stage.

Mrs Roberts put the medal around her neck. 'Congratulations, Ruby, you did a truly wonderful thing.'

'Thank you.'

Ruby looked out at the school. Everyone was clapping and cheering; Safa, Clara and Denise were whooping. Safa must have told Orla about the award because she had come over from the senior school and was standing at the back of the hall, doing her loud wolf whistle.

Amber and Chrissie were the only ones not cheering, but Ruby didn't care.

She whispered in Mrs Roberts' ear.

Mrs Roberts held up her hands. 'Girls, before you go, Ruby would like to say a few words.'

Ruby stepped forward. She wasn't sure what she was going to say, but then she looked at Safa and she knew.

'This isn't really my award. This should have been given to my best friend, Safa. She's the brave one. She had to run away from her country because of the big war and planes dropping bombs. Her cat died and her school was bombed and she had to travel in a dark truck and go across the sea in a little boat full of people who hadn't a clue where they were going. She got stuck in Greece in a camp – not like a cool campsite – a horrible one where you have to queue for, like, ages to get food and the food you get is horrible.

'When Miss Ingle told me I had to look after her on her first day, four months ago, I was really cross. I didn't want to have to look after anyone. I was so selfish. I feel bad about that. I didn't know then that Safa would become my absolute best friend. I didn't know then that she would come into my family and make everything better. I felt sorry for myself because I have a brother with disabilities, but when I heard all the bad things that had happened to Safa I knew that my problems weren't all that big.

'But even though she had all those problems and her dad was missing and they couldn't find him, she still thought about me and my family and she is the reason Robbie is going to a really good school and everything is going to be good again. Safa is the bravest person I know. She's also the kindest and most generous person. She has so little, but she gives so much.

'I know we're really different and all, but actually in a way we're not. We were both sad about stuff when we met and then we both helped each other to fix our problems. I am so glad I was able to help find her dad, but Clara and Denise were brilliant too.'

'Yes we were!' Clara shouted.

'I agree!' Denise laughed.

Ruby smiled at them. 'Safa has shown me that even though things might seem really bad, you have to look at the good side of life. You have to look at what you do have and be thankful. She's also shown me that you can help people, even if you're only a kid. If you're determined and brave, you can do anything.

'So I'm sharing this award with my best friend, Safa.'

Everyone cheered loudly and clapped. Ruby ran down from the stage and hugged Safa. Best friends, who had helped make each other's lives better by being brave and kind-hearted.

'Thanks for finding my dad.'

'Thanks for getting Robbie into school.'

'I'm so glad you were asked to look after me on that first day.' Safa wiped away a tear.

'Me too.' Ruby sniffed.

They beamed at each other. Two girls who were

lost in their own way, suffering in silence, who came together and helped each other heal.

Two girls from opposite ends of the world, who decided to help each other, and changed their lives for ever.

Further information

n 1998, Ireland was one of the first six countries in Europe to set up a resettlement programme. The Irish Refugee Resettlement Programme has been in operation since 2000 and is run by the Irish government in collaboration with UNHCR (the United Nations Refugee Agency). Under this resettlement programme, refugees who cannot go home because of war or fear of persecution and who live in dangerous situations or have specific needs may be resettled. Between 2000 and 2019, over 3,000 refugees from almost 30 nations were resettled in Ireland.

In 2015 the Irish government created the Irish Refugee Protection Programme (IRPP) to manage the resettlement of refugees fleeing conflict in the Middle East and Africa. Since 2015, Ireland has accepted nearly 3,800 people under the IRPP. Under the first phase of the Irish Refugee Protection Programme, 1,022 asylum seekers came to Ireland from Greece. (In this book, the character Safa and her mum come to Ireland under this programme.)

If you are interested in learning more about refugees and resettlement programmes, here are some websites you can look up:

☆ www.unhcr.org/en-ie/
☆ www.irishrefugeecouncil.ie

- ☆ www.justice.ie/en/JELR/Pages/Irish_Refugee_Protection_Programme_(IRPP)
- ☆ www.schools-ireland.cityofsanctuary.org/

Acknowledgements

Having published fifteen adult novels, this is my first foray into the world of children's books and I have enjoyed every single minute. This book has been a passion project for me. I wrote it to try to help children to understand the plight of refugees. It's hard for kids to understand what it's like for a refugee child to find themselves in a different country. I want to help children to be able to walk a mile in someone else's shoes. With Safa and Ruby's story, I hope to show children how important kindness and compassion are. There is so much power in a kind word and a helping hand.

I have lots of people to thank for getting this book out into the world:

My agent Marianne Gunn O'Connor, who believed in the book from the beginning. She has been such a champion and friend. Thank you from the bottom of my heart.

Thank you, Deirdre Nolan, for your passion about *The New Girl* and for 'getting' what I was trying to achieve with this novel.

And to all the team at Gill, you have been wonderful to work with.

To Nick Henderson, CEO of the Irish Refugee Council, for being so supportive of *The New Girl* and for the information you have provided on refugees and how to help.

Thank you to Hannah Culkin, who I contacted a few years ago when she worked for Doras and who put me in touch with the wonderful Sarra al-Hariri.

Sarra and her family are Syrian refugees who came to Ireland a few years ago. Sarra is a beautiful, elegant and bright young woman. When I first met her she was studying for her Leaving Cert and we sat down and talked for hours. She told me her story of being smuggled to freedom and talked about her experiences of being a refugee in Ireland. I have since met her sisters, Taqwa and Amira, and her lovely mum Fatima. This book is dedicated to Sarra, who has become a dear friend and is a brave and brilliant young woman.

A huge thank you to my three wonderful children, Hugo, Geordy and Amy, who all read and edited this book. They gave me invaluable feedback and helped shape the book. An extra-special thanks to Amy, who kept telling me not to give up and reassuring me that the book would be published.

Thanks to Troy for being my rock.

To my mum, who wrote non-fiction children's books about Irish historical figures when I was growing up, thanks for leading the way.